FLYNN

N GRAY

VINCI BOOKS

FLYNN

N. GRAY

VINCI
BOOKS

By N Gray

The Dana Mulder Suspense Thriller Series

Deadly Pattern

Devil Mountain

Chasing Evil

Nightcrawler

Horror

What's for Dinner

Creature Features

Monster Features

Thrillers

Lady Killer

More from N Gray

writing as Natalie Michaels

Steve Campbell Psychological Suspense Thrillers

The Last Girl

The Bone Forest

The White Dahlia

I See You

Death in the City

More from N Gray

writing as SD Syns

The Diaries

Red Lace Diaries

www.ngraybooks.com

Vinci Books

vinci-books.com

Published by Vinci Books Ltd in 2026

1

The publisher and the author have made every effort to obtain permissions
for any third party material used in this book and to comply with copyright
law. Any queries in this respect should be brought to the attention of the
publisher and any omissions will be corrected in future editions.
A CIP catalogue record for this book is available from the British Library.
Paperback ISBN: 9781036702267
The EU GPSR authorised representative is Logos Europe, 9 rue Nicolas
Poussion, 17000 La Rochelle, France contact@logoseurope.eu

Chapter One

Dwayne combed his dirty fingers through his greasy hair as he watched Natalie and Penn laugh. He loved the way the flames cast their beautiful features in shades of red and yellow, reminding him of a painting he had on his wall.

Dwayne pulled his ruffled shirt down, tucked it into his pants and pulled it out again. The shirt was uncomfortable, and he silently cursed his servant for not ironing his clothing the way he specified. He would have another talk with her when he got home.

Twigs snapped behind him and he flinched. He moved deeper into the shadows of the forest, pushing leaves to one side and smiled. Penn had her back to him as she picked food off the plate.

Dwayne adjusted his crotch, thinking about Penn and Natalie in his company like before, remembering a time when all they had was each other. It was a dark time for them, but he escaped, too, and he had forgiven them for leaving him to die.

Voices traveled closer to his hiding spot and Dwayne

1

stopped breathing. His nictitating eyelid moved when he blinked. His forked tongue tasted the air; leopards. He resisted the urge to hiss and give away his location.

No. He needed to wait. Wait until the girls were alone before doing what he wanted. And this time, nobody would escape.

Chapter Two

I wiped my face with my right hand and scratched my beard, but my fingers got caught in the caked blood; I needed to shower.

Glancing at the fading bruises, it relieved me the cuts were healing, leaving behind dried blood on my now smooth skin.

I glanced at my swollen eyes as visions of the carnage flashed before me; blood, torn flesh, and body parts. Then distant memories echoed with moans from those hurt, followed by screaming and shrieking.

The events that had just taken place would haunt me forever.

I glanced up when Jude entered the bathroom, giving me same expression I gave him; a *'what the fuck did we just go through?'* look.

I couldn't recall the fight with Shannon all those years ago being this gruesome, but it was Shannon's offspring who had caused the fight today; which was just as bad, if not worse.

Shannon reminded me of a mad scientist; he mixed various DNA of a human and a shifter animal to create supernatural hybrids. They started off as his children, until he locked them up in cages like animals, because he wanted supernatural soldiers who were his killing machines instead.

I shook my head, grateful Shannon was no more, but the son he created had followed in his footsteps. Like evil father, like evil son; I shuddered at the thought.

"How are you holding up?" Jude asked, his tone gentle, throwing his towel over his naked shoulder.

"I'll get through it," I said and tried to smile, but I wasn't fooling him. "How's Lee?" I asked, changing the subject.

"He's with Sebastian at the Leap. The leopards who followed Dwayne to his location have returned and they're busy devising a plan to get the sisters back safely."

Dwayne had kidnapped Natalie and Penn, his sisters, right from under our noses. Even with all the were-leopards there, and us, we couldn't defend the sisters against him. But he wasn't alone. Dwayne had an army of hybrid Komodo dragons on his side, and he could command them to do as he pleased.

We didn't have a chance to shift into our stronger beasts. When the first were-leopard went down, shriveled into a husk and died, I realized we didn't have a fighting chance; their venomous bites killed us quickly.

One thing everyone agreed to was that we couldn't leave the sisters with the madman. It wasn't in my DNA not to help, but the thought of going through another battle left me on edge. I'd experienced enough death and destruction to last me ten life times. Yet, I had to help Lee get Natalie and Penn back, even if it cost me.

When I didn't respond, Jude added, "All the shifters are

banding together." His tone was gentler. "They say Dwayne took the girls to the lab where Shannon had created them and his army. We're leaving tonight," he said with hard lines etched into his face.

Jude and I had been through a lot together, and this was one fight I didn't want him to go on without me.

We moved to Sterling Meadow round about the same time. He had no tiger clan to join, so he joined me and the lions with Troy's permission.

Then we started working for Léon, the Master Vampire of Sterling Meadow, in his warehouse and had been friends since. Plus, we're always with Kai and Lee, so their leopards always included us in their meetings and parties.

It wasn't just the shifters protecting the town, but the vampires under Léon's rule, too. Everybody joined forces to keep everyone safe from danger. Léon was one of the nicest vampires to work for, and one of the best supernaturals who wouldn't hesitate to help. He did whatever it took to ensure we were all out of harm's way.

And because of my work relationship with Léon, I now had a brother in Jude, Lee, and Kai. The four of us worked together, lived together, and protected each other. That was the main reason why I couldn't let Lee down. I had to help him get Natalie back; even if it cost me my sanity.

"You don't have to do this—"

"No, I'll go. We all do," I said, turning around. "Everyone would help me if I was in Lee's shoes."

"Yes," Jude said, shrugging. "But he didn't wake up in a pool of his mother's blood. You did. Everyone knows you have triggers."

I shook my head, expelling the memory of the slaughter I had found myself in when I was ten years old. My village had been destroyed, and all my people were butchered. My head was almost split in two, yet I survived with my mother's corpse on top of me, protecting me from blows meant for me.

"I have to help."

Jude grabbed my shoulder and squeezed. "You can join me in the back. We'll be protecting the first wave." He smiled sadly. "Then, once they're through, we'll hold back for any Komodo dragons trying to escape. We're better prepared this time." He smiled sinisterly, and it brought a smile to my face. When Jude behaved like this, he had something up his sleeve; and whatever *it* was, I knew it would kill the dragons before they reached us.

"You should shower, too." Jude hung his towel up and stepped into the open shower. "Get that muck off your skin."

Chapter Three

I combed my fingers through my short, clean hair as the hot water cascaded down my back, leaving a trail of goosebumps in its wake. The soap had rinsed through long ago, but I wasn't ready to get out, I was enjoying the sensation of the water massaging my muscles; the cuts and bruises had healed as if nothing had happened. I sighed wearily and turned the tap off, grabbing my towel and slowly dried my body.

"Hey, man. Are you okay?" Jude asked, wearing black cargo pants and a top so tight it outlined his muscles.

"You going clubbing?"

"Ha, funny." He smiled. "They're waiting for us outside." He didn't leave, instead he stared at me. He knew I was procrastinating. "Are you sure you want to come?"

I nodded. "Yes, give me ten minutes." I darted past him to my room, towel dried as fast as I could, and slipped on similar black combat gear.

The memories of being crushed by my mother, holding my breath, and shutting my eyes tight hit me at once…

"Play dead," Mom said.

Those were her last words to me before she died. Her arms were wrapped around me, protecting me as she slowly fell into a forever sleep.

And that's what I did; for two days and nights I stayed there, pretending to be dead until I was sure nobody else was around. My village was a cemetery, and nobody was going to rescue me.

I flinched when Jude slapped the doorframe, jolting me back to reality. He said nothing but I nodded my understanding, pulled on my boots, and grabbed my rifle.

We exited the warehouse where two of Léon's vampires waited for us. They would watch the place while we were out killing Komodo dragons. They nodded curtly, entered the enormous building, and slammed the door shut.

We didn't wait outside for long when we heard the vehicle before we saw it. I watched this chunky piece of metal on wheels and felt better already.

Lee pulled up in an armored vehicle he borrowed from a military connection he had. The determination in his eyes was enough to restore my strength as hope filled my veins. I forgot about my devastating childhood and focused on a future where my brother got his woman back.

Lee stopped the vehicle and thumbed behind him, and without saying a word, we climbed inside. Kai sat beside Lee, a silent pillar of strength, and the atmosphere inside the cabin shot up a notch. When I closed the heavy door, Lee smashed the gas, taking off like his ass was on fire.

We met up with every shifter who lived in and around Sterling Meadow and Krystal Creek. There were some were-animals who had already shifted into their beast, while some remained in human form and armed themselves with weapons to destroy the Komodo dragons under Dwayne's command.

"The ammunition is something the military has been working on since Shannon created his little army of super-humans," Lee said, handing Jude and me a box each. "Apparently, it comprises some type of acid that, upon impact with the creatures, will start eating their skin and their skin only. Leaving us unharmed—"

"Have you tested this?" Kai asked, sliding in the magazine.

"What do you think?" Lee said, smirking. "I'll never let you guys use something I can't confirm won't hurt us. You're like brothers to me."

"Just don't choke up and shed a tear," Jude joked. "Let's get this party started."

The vehicle moved slowly forward through the rough terrain; the sound of tree branches scraping against the sides of the vehicle reminding me of a horror.

We headed toward the mountain where Shannon once had his lab. The old road was barely visible now that parts of the forest had covered it. It felt like forever since we were last here, but it was only a few years ago.

It didn't take long for the fight to start. Something large flew in the air, but Lee was quick enough and stopped the vehicle before an enormous boulder crushed us. The boulder stopped dead in the ground, lifting grass, instead of rolling onto us which was a blessing; it would shelter us for a moment while we gathered our bearings.

The four of us surveyed the dark scenery in search of attacking Komodo dragons, but there were none. They were either waiting for us to get out or they had another plan.

I squinted into the darkness, searching for strange shapes. There atop a cliff stood a Komodo/human hybrid; from the waist down, he was a Komodo dragon, but from the chest up he was very male. Someone had spotted him and shone a torch on his face, his black, dead eyes were focused on us. I doubted there was a brain that worked on its own, but instead, driven by a mad-man.

"What the hell happened to the creatures?" Jude asked, his jaw slacken.

The Komodo dragons that had attacked us earlier were only dragons, not this hybrid type. I suspected Dwayne had kept these ones back in case we retaliated.

"When I spoke to my contact at the military, he told me they'd been tracking Dwayne for years until he evaded them. And as we suspected, he studied his father's recipe and replicated the experiments; creating Komodo dragon hybrids as his own private foot soldiers. Don't worry, they'll be the easiest to kill," Lee said gravely, killing the engine and opening his door.

Lights from other vehicles had stopped behind us, illuminating at least a thousand shifters in various fighting stances standing ready to attack.

We climbed out of the vehicle and stood beside Lee. We waited, watching for movement in the darkness. There was no moon to light our way, but there were flashlights bright enough for us to recognize shapes in the blackest areas, and channeled our inner-animal hearing for signs of activity.

We didn't wait long.

The first angry Komodo dragon slithered across the floor quickly. Its poisonous tongue tasting the air as it charged us. Those powerful jaws needed to snap bones in two and eat one of us; it needed blood.

We didn't wait for them to get close again, not like last time. We aimed our weapons and fired.

The Komodo charging me didn't get close enough to hurt me. I fired, the bullet struck, and it crashed instantly. Its eye popped and pus oozed out of the wound, while the head wound melted inside its skull.

We killed them all within minutes. Each special bullet hitting a Komodo dragon and it sunk into their tough flesh, eating them from the inside. Some bullets obliterated powerful jaws, but it didn't stop eating its victim until there was nothing left but mushed, bubbling flesh on the ground.

We stood watching them die one after the other until there was nothing left but limbs twitching in the darkness. When shrieks and cries sounded from inside the mountain, followed by cursing, we surmised that it was Dwayne realizing we had destroyed his Komodo pets.

A whistle sounded and a second wave of Komodo dragon hybrids rushed us. Again, the attack didn't last as we took them out, too. They didn't have a chance against our powerful ammunition. They were all left to wither and die in their ruined bodies while their minds tried to comprehend what happened to them.

When the last hybrid crashed to the ground, the only thing I heard was my breathing and heartbeat. I wiped sweat off my face with the back of my hand and enjoyed the cool caress of the wind against my skin.

The darkness of the night seemed to shift into something else, too, something better, lighter, like the world knew what had gone on inside that mountain and could now breathe with relief once more.

Now we had to find Dwayne, kill him, and get the sisters back. I hoped this was the end of him and there were no surprises.

The men beside me spoke among themselves, but I tuned them out. I glanced down at my hands, at the veins bulging, and it relieved me I didn't need to use excessive force to destroy the Komodo dragons, but more importantly none of the shifters were hurt. As much as I enjoyed shifting into my beasts, I was glad it wasn't necessary and there was no blood staining my skin.

The voices died down and I glanced up. Jude stayed beside me while Lee and Kai walked toward the mountain. They entered the caves and I shivered in the cool breeze. Some of the shifters joined them and searched the area.

Jude and I waited in comfortable silence and after half an hour, the two men exited the mountain with a swagger. I only saw their silhouette but the moment two figures became four, I smiled.

As Lee and Kai reached us with the two sisters, the mountain rumbled as the lab exploded preventing anyone from going inside again.

Chapter Four

I sat at the breakfast table, pushing my food from one side of the plate to the other.

Lee and Natalie sat glued to each other. They had only been together a week but they were made for each other. I could practically see loving stars in their eyes.

I didn't blame them for not letting the other out of their sights. If I ever found *the one* and someone kidnapped her, I'd do the same.

Kai and Naomi were newlyweds and in his room up to all sorts of mischief; I wouldn't tell them breakfast was being served and they should hurry. If they wanted to eat food, they would be here.

Jude was patrolling the perimeter of the warehouse.

Penn, Natalie's sister, sat on the opposite side of the table. She tried desperately to look busy by reading the only magazine we had in the warehouse.

I watched Penn for a moment too long and she glanced up, her brows furrowing. "Quit staring at me," she mumbled, her angry eyes still on mine.

I raised my hands. "Did you have enough to eat?" I asked, raising the bowl of scrambled eggs.

She nodded and continued reading the same page she'd been on since I sat down.

Lee and Natalie stopped kissing and glanced between Penn and me.

"Why don't you guys—"

"No!" Penn yelled, slamming the magazine on the table and stood. "Don't set me up with anyone," — she pointed at me, — "especially not a lion. I don't want to do anything with anyone or date right now."

"Penn?" Natalie said gently and reached for her sister. As Natalie touched Penn's hand, Penn pulled away and ran out of the kitchen. "Sorry about that, Flynn. She's been through a lot."

"Don't worry about it. I understand," I said, removing the dishes from the table and packed them in the dishwasher.

Penn had been through enough to make a grown man cry. A year ago, a witch had cursed her, forcing her to stay in her Komodo dragon animal. For a year, she remained in her beast until last week when Natalie reversed the curse, making Penn human again. Then, just as she tasted freedom, Dwayne kidnapped her.

That's how Lee and Natalie met; he helped her retrieve the egg that reversed the curse.

Natalie said nothing had happened to them physically while in Dwayne's company, but I suspected Penn may need some form of therapy. But it wasn't up to me to suggest anything. Natalie could bring it up if she thought her sister needed it.

"You and Jude off duty tonight?" Lee asked, bringing me out of my thoughts.

"Oh, yeah," I said, closing the dishwasher and pressing start.

"You going out?"

"Nah," I said, shaking my head and drying my hands on a dishtowel. "Think I'll have an early night. I'm exhausted."

"They say it might snow tonight."

That caught my attention. "It's not that time of year."

"I know," Lee said. "It's not cold enough either."

"Well, I hope it does snow. I think we all need a change of scenery."

"I agree," Natalie said, joining the conversation. "Penn loves snow. Hopefully, it brings her out of her bad mood." She leaned her head against Lee's shoulder then sat upright. "Come," she said, standing and reached for Lee's hand. "I want to lie down before your shift starts."

I chuckled when Lee's grin split his face in two. I'd never seen the leopard smile so much before. Young love was the best; everything was new, exciting, and filled with so many possibilities.

Lee climbed to his feet and followed Natalie out.

It was my turn to clean the kitchen, and I took my time doing so; it was therapeutic wiping the tables and washing the frying pan in a slow continuous motion.

My heavy heart finally started to lift as I consciously let go of last week's carnage. It rarely took me this long to get over a fight, but the visuals of the destroyed Komodo dragon hybrids was enough to push anyone over the edge. Yet, it didn't affect many, only those who were highly sensitive; like myself, and like Penn.

When my kitchen duty was over, I decided to go for a walk and pulled on a fresh shirt and jacket. As I stepped outside, the warehouse door slamming shut, a snowflake floated near my face, followed by a few thousand more. Lee was right… snow.

I zipped up my jacket and walked block after block until I reached the edge of the forest that surrounded Sterling Meadow; this part was for everyone. Many years ago, when more shifters moved to town, they needed to separate each were-animal to avoid fighting; wolves, leopards, rats, and lions. So they divided up the forest into equal parts, and they left this section for the trolls, faeries, and any other supernatural creature in need of a home.

I hadn't ventured into these parts in years. I was always in the were-lions part of the forest, and sometimes with the leopards.

My lion clan, led by Troy, was the third largest shifter group in Sterling Meadow, second were the leopards led by Sebastian, and the largest by far were the wolves run by Shawn.

Shawn managed his wolves like a CEO, and nobody did anything without his knowledge. If they did, everyone in the Were-Animal Alliance, WAA, ensured it didn't happen again.

That's what I loved about my town. We were different, yet when there was danger or someone was in trouble, we banded together. Our community looked after each other; including the vampires.

I'd lived in a few cities and towns, but none came close to this type of camaraderie. That's why I'd never leave this place. It was my home.

I traversed deeper into the forest; dark shadows painted the trees sinisterly. The snow continued falling around me, coating branches and brushes with a soft white layer. The sun disappeared behind thick gray clouds and a shudder ran through me like a blade running down my spine.

I stopped in my tracks and glanced up ahead, squinting at the trees and branches. A gentle wind caressed the uncovered leaves, and some branches swayed.

I sniffed the air; mold and sewage. I was in the forest and that combination of stink shouldn't be here, yet it was overwhelming.

Unsure of who or what was nearby, I opted to blend with the shadows until I knew for sure. I pulled my black hoody up over my head; grateful my beard was dark, or they'd be able to see my pale jawline.

Leaves crunched to my right. I sucked in my breath. The footsteps edged closer. The sounds stopped; not an insect was heard with snowflakes floating to the already soaked ground.

My heart thundered in my chest. I squared my stance as I readied for an attack. I waited.

The steps started again, quicker this time; like they were running away from someone; or running toward someone. I didn't want to get caught in the middle of their fight. If there was an outside group entering our territory, we would've heard about it through the WAA, and I couldn't recall hearing such news. But with everything that had happened this week, anything was possible.

I waited. The footsteps neared. Twigs snapped, leaves crunched, then a loud thump, followed by moaning.

"Fuck!" she moaned.

I frowned, stepping out from under the shadows and into the midday gloom as snow continued falling. The stench of mold and sewage was now gone.

I stared at the person on all fours and stifled a laugh. "What are you doing out here, Penn?" I asked as I reached to help her up.

"Get away from me, lion," she growled, waving me away.

"What is your problem with lions, or is it me?" I asked, stepping away from her.

Penn rocked onto her haunches, then stood on wobbly legs. She rubbed her temples and breathed deeply. Glancing down, Penn swiped leaves and dirt from her pants, then glared daggers in my direction. "You. Lions. Shifters. You're all the same to me—"

"I did nothing to you. So wrap that bitchiness up tight and direct it toward someone deserving. I helped to get you away from Dwayne."

"I don't care. Which way out of the godforsaken forest?" She said in a huff.

"Na-hah, princess. You can't talk to me that way and expect me to help you." I stomped away from her and in the mountain's direction. If she followed me, she'd get an easy way back to the warehouse. I would not allow her the satisfaction of being cruel to me and getting her way. It would please me in making it difficult for her to find her way back to the warehouse.

I heard her following me, and I couldn't help but shake my head and smirk at her audacity. I didn't know what her problem was, but I wouldn't play into her hands either.

"This isn't the way to the warehouse," Penn grumbled behind me. "You've just taken us farther into the forest."

I spun around and pointed a finger at her. "You've made it abundantly clear you don't like me. Therefore, you're not my responsibility. So go away." I shooed her away. "Complain into someone's ear who actually cares. You've been offish toward me for an entire week, so from today onward I'm done with you." I spun around and started running away from her.

My actions were painfully childish, but I didn't care. I was having some fun with a girl who needed to lighten up. Yes, she had a rough time, and I should take it easy on her, but she needed to get out of her funky mood. And, in my opinion, laughter was the best way to achieve that.

The snow fell harder, wetting my face and shoulders. The faster I ran, the faster Penn ran behind me. We ran at that speed for a while when I heard laughter, followed by another hard thud.

I stopped in my tracks and glanced over my shoulder at Penn sitting on the wet ground, her clothing muddy, laughing hysterically. Her laughter made me smile, and I closed the gap. When I reached her, I proffered a hand.

Penn glanced up at me, her smile was still there, and after a moment's hesitation, grabbed my hand. I carefully pulled her to her feet, but she lost balance and I caught her before she fell to the floor again.

I caught Penn at such a weird angle that her cheek was pressed against my chest, and her hands were holding onto my biceps like her life depended on it. She quickly let go and stepped away from me. I didn't want to make a scene of something innocent, so I ignored how good she felt against me or that she was embarrassed.

"Are you okay?" I asked, checking to see if she had any wounds.

"I'm fine." She wiped her muddy hands on her pants. "I tripped over a root or something." She exhaled and shook out her shoulders. "Where are we anyway?" She asked, glancing at the large oak trees surrounding us.

"Uhm, I've never been this far out before." I glanced around and didn't recognize any part of it, and the mountain was still in the distance. "Let's go the way we came." I pointed at the path we'd just used.

"Does this mean we're heading back now?" she said with a sly smirk and shivered. She rubbed her shoulders and her bottom lip trembled; her jacket was paper thin.

"Here," I said, unzipping my jacket.

"No, please, keep your jacket on."

"Penn, I insist. I'm not cold, but your lips are turning blue." I pointed at her chattering jaw. She was freezing. "So please put it on before you die out here. I really don't want your sister blaming me for your death."

"Thank you," she smiled timidly, pulling on my jacket, and sighing with relief. Penn huddled into herself and walked beside me as we headed back the same way we came. "Your jacket is really warm. This last week I've been back in my human form has been weird. I think my body is still getting used to my thin skin. I'm always cold."

"Have you shifted into your Komodo dragon again?"

"Oh hell no," she said, shaking her head. "I'm scared I won't be able to change back again. I don't think I'd be able to handle another year like that."

I didn't blame Penn for feeling that way, and she needed to get used to living in her human skin again. Being stuck in her thick-skinned Komodo dragon for a year would do that to her. Unfortunately, shifters didn't survive something like that and remain sane. Of the stories I had heard, when a shifter was stuck or cursed to remain in their animal, they usually killed themselves or were killed by hunters. Or they ran off into the forest, never to be seen again.

Penn was incredibly lucky her sister communicated telepathically with her during the ordeal and she found her way back to her Natalie. Unfortunately, the sisters had to be in close proximity for it to work. So for now Penn couldn't reach out to her sister and was my responsibility to get home safely.

As we hiked through the forest, I noted the footpath we had used earlier didn't look familiar, and the scenery seemed different from moments before. I couldn't shake the feeling we were lost.

I stopped and glanced up; the sun had shifted and the sky was darkening. We were heading in the right direction, but I couldn't tell if we were closer to town. I had no watch but if the sun was any indication we had been walking around for quite a few hours.

The snow continued falling, forming layers on the trees, bushes, and on the ground. Our feet crunched deeper into the snow, wetting our boots and pants. The wind had picked up, whipping snowflakes across our cheeks.

"We need to find shelter," I said, huddling into myself. When I turned toward Penn, her lips were still blue and her face ashen. "When last did you eat?"

Her chin moved, but no words came out. She shook her head.

"Come," I said, grabbing her elbow. "We need to find shelter until the blizzard blows over."

I think Penn nodded her approval. She didn't object to me manhandling her either, so I continued pulling her in the direction of a cave I'd spotted.

"Here," I said, pointing at the first opening. "This should be fine."

Chapter Five

Penn entered the cave ahead of me and stopped dead. "I can't see in the dark," she whispered, reaching out for my hand.

I led her to one side of the cave while I ran back out into the snow. I grabbed the driest branches and leaves I could find and enough to build a fire that would hopefully last the evening.

Luckily, I found untouched wood and stacked them against the wall of the cave. Once the fire was lit, I cleared the ground for Penn to sit.

"Thank you," she said. She remained quiet for a heartbeat then added, "Sorry for being such a bitch to you." Penn sat down, sighing frustratingly. "My behavior isn't because you're a lion, and as cliche as it sounds, it's because I like you, but I'm still skeptical about whom to trust." She glanced up at me. The pain of her experience shone brightly in her eyes.

Natalie had told me Penn had trusted her friends, but

they were the ones who took her directly to the witch who had cursed her. They met their demise but that didn't change the fact she had been betrayed.

I nodded and sat across from her. The delicate oranges and reds from the scorching fire splashed across her smooth, pale skin, brightening her features. She was beautiful in a fragile way.

"I can only imagine what you've gone through. But," — I shrugged, — "we've all lived a life and gone through some type of trauma. We all have a story to share, and try to pick up the pieces and move on." I cleared my throat and got comfortable.

Penn stared at me, waiting for more.

"Take myself, for instance," I continued. "I take it one day at a time, and I only do what I'm able to do. I force nothing on myself. I focus on one task at hand and do it the best I can, without dumping my trauma on someone else. One never knows what that person is going through."

The lines between her eyes deepened, the fire highlighting her features in warm light. She was breathtakingly beautiful once the hardness of her walls softened, and she allowed someone inside.

"They slaughtered my family when I was about ten years old," I said, not looking at her. "Men in black cloaks entered our village and killed everyone before we defended ourselves. Till today I don't understand why, but my mother did everything in her power to protect me." I swallowed hard at the memory. "And there's nobody I can speak to because everyone is gone." I blinked back tears.

"It's okay. If it's too hard, you don't have to say more," Penn said gently.

I smiled sadly. "I want to tell you. I want you to understand that it's okay to share your pain." My smile lingered but I knew the pain in my eyes was enough for her to understand.

"My mother protected me. She ensured they couldn't find me beneath her bloodied body. I lay under her corpse for two, almost three days, unmoving. All I did was breathe and sleep. I didn't open my eyes until I was sure nobody was around. On the third day, I did just that, I pushed my mother's body off and I sat up. I was weak, exhausted, and mourning for my mother and my people."

I stood up the moment the rush of emotions flooded my system with painful memories. Pacing helped, but I knew I had to continue the story. It was therapeutic for me to share what I'd gone through, and hopefully let go of the hurt that was paralyzing me.

"They destroyed my entire village. The were-lions never had a chance to fight back. I didn't see much of what had happened, but I heard my people's screams. I do remember they wore black cloaks." I shrugged nonchalantly.

"I'm so sorry, Flynn. That's awful." Penn stood up and approached me. Without waiting for a response, she wrapped her slender arms around my waist and pressed her body against mine. Her hug brought warmth to my chest and soul, and I held her tightly.

We were two wounded souls with lasting pain. We didn't want to fix the other, just allow ourselves to feel the emotions. Then, when our shared moment ended, we would continue on our own healing journey.

Penn let go first, and I stepped away from her. Her eyes held unshed tears. Whether it was for me or herself, I didn't know nor did I want to ask, but we shared something special in that moment.

"Let it out," I said, staring deeply into her eyes. When I thumbed a rogue tear from her cheek, she let go of the hurt she'd been carrying around like baggage. She cried until there were no more tears left, and I held her until she was ready to stand on her own.

Chapter Six

I kept the fire hot while the snow continued falling; there was at least three inches of snow covering the ground at the entrance of the cave already.

Penn had fallen asleep, warmly tucked in with my jacket. It relieved me she was at least warm, but I knew we had to get out of here as soon as possible.

Being a shifter, my core body temperature remained five degrees higher than a human, but Penn's seemed to be much lower. I surmised it was because of the reptilian part of her being cold-blooded. It could also explain why she wasn't eating much, but she needed to keep up her strength. I hadn't seen her eat at all this last week.

Luckily, I was a large burley man with muscles to keep me warm, but I'd only stay warm for a short time while out in the snow. But we needed food to keep up our strength, and I needed to be quick.

I exited the warmth of the cave and shivered as the snow melted against my skin. I cast my eye across the forest, waiting. Something scuttled across the ground and up a tree.

I darted after it. I loved all creatures, but we needed suste-nance. It physically pained me to do this.

I caught the squirrel before it could disappear farther up the tree. As I headed back toward the cave, a tiny fox stared at me. My heart dropped to my stomach; I didn't want to eat a fox, but I didn't know how long we'd be stuck in the cave. I'd forgotten to take my cellphone when I pulled on my jacket and Penn hadn't been around long enough to get herself one, yet.

The fox continued giving me that look that told me he was not food. He was right, I couldn't do it. We'd make do with the squirrel. The sooner we returned to the warehouse, the better.

When I entered the cave, Penn was adding wood to the fire.

"I hope you're hungry?" I asked, handing her the tiny creature.

"Thanks," she said, her smile lingering. "You want to share?"

"I ate breakfast, you didn't. It's all yours." I added another twig to the flames and scooted closer, warming my damp body.

Penn didn't bother cooking it. She opened her mouth, her forked tongue tasting the furry creature, and her jaw unlatched. Scales spread across her skin as she partially shifted. Her eyes glowed a swampy green color and her third eyelid closed and opened as she blinked.

I'd seen crocodile shifters, but never a Komodo dragon, and none so pretty. Penn was nothing like the hybrid Komodo-dragon-killing-machines we'd seen. They were stiff-looking rugrats who were unnaturally human and far from Komodo. They only had one thing going for them, that their bites killed instantly, but they were riddled with flaws that got them killed.

Penn was breathtakingly perfect. To a human, I was sure she'd scare the crap out of them while she ate. I'd love to see her in her glorious Komodo dragon form, and then laugh watching the human crowds scatter. For shifters like me, we would embrace her difference; even appreciate it.

For now, I'd happily watch her eat a squirrel whole. She chewed a few times on that tiny creature then swallowed satisfactory. Her scales returned to porcelain skin and her eyes bled back to their usual green color. She tucked dark strands of hair behind her ears when she realized I was watching.

I didn't take my eyes off her. I wanted her to feel my dark gaze. She needed to know she could come out of the darkness and into the light, and I'd be there to remind her how to live again. That she was desirable, even if it was someone like me.

I scratched my now dry beard.

"Have you always had a beard?" Penn asked, her cheeks rosy.

"No, I started growing it this year." I sat against the wall of the cave and closer to Penn. "Do you think I should shave?"

"No," — her eyes flitted to the fire, then back at me, — "I like it. But shave… if you want."

"No, I think I'll keep it." I smirked and stretched out my legs that almost touched her feet.

"Luckily, you got enough wood. Are you dry enough?"

"I'm fine, thanks."

We sat in comfortable silence. Penn's attention went from the snow falling outside to the warm fire while I watched Penn.

Chapter Seven

I awoke with a start, bolting upright, then stood. My hackles raised and my sharp teeth elongating. I moved closer to the mouth of the cave and peered outside; the glare of snow reflected brightly. I raised my left arm to shade my eyes as I stared out into the white forest.

Someone was outside in the snow watching us. I felt their dark gaze on me. My thoughts crashed to Penn and glanced in her direction. She sat up, sensing danger herself, and shook her head as if reading my thoughts. We sensed someone out there. I didn't like it.

Penn stood beside me. I wrapped an arm around her shoulders and brought her closer. We stood like statues and stared at the white wall of snow falling outside the cave.

The snow had packed tightly at the mouth of the cave, creating a step. It relieved me it hadn't fallen inside the cave too much; instead, it created a protective barrier keeping most of the snow outside.

Waves of goosebumps crawled over my skin, and I

didn't like the sensation. Whoever was outside was not a friendly.

On instinct, I pushed Penn behind me. She obliged and curled her fingers through my jean belt loops.

The snow moved unnaturally near the entrance of the cave. I narrowed my eyes at the snowflakes forming a shoulder. I squeezed Penn's hips, keeping her in place, and stepped us farther into the darkness of the cave.

"I mean no harm." His voice was husky. The translucent shoulder materialized into a man wearing white from head to toe, sporting a white goatee and a head full of white hair. His dark blue eyes were warm and welcoming when he saw us. "You won't survive in this cave for long and the snow isn't letting up. If you like, you're welcoming to follow me to my village," he said, stepping closer.

When I flinched, he stopped moving.

"My name is Aziir. My clan is literally around the corner from here." He smiled kindly.

"I've never heard of a clan inside these woods." My tone was harsh.

"We've hidden ourselves from everyone. But I assure you, there are no fences to keep you prisoner, so you can leave when you're ready. But if I were you, I wouldn't stay here. At this rate," — he nodded at the falling snow, — "it will cover the entrance soon and stop you from hunting or gathering firewood." Aziir turned and headed for the exit. "We can offer warm clothing, too." He nodded at Penn, who now stood beside me, shivering. "Come," he said. "I mean no harm and offer shelter."

Chapter Eight

Before heading out, Aziir offered me a top, which I reluctantly accepted and was pleasantly surprised it fit my larger build and it kept me warm in the cold.

Penn kept to my left-hand side, slipping her hand through mine. She was quiet, but I knew she was thinking, as was I; this stranger arriving at our cave offering us shelter and food was too convenient. But we didn't have a choice until the blizzard stopped.

I sensed Aziir was a shaman; his power oozed out of his pores and surrounded him in a soft orange glaze. I didn't know how potent his power was, but suspected it was great.

The beads around his neck clinked together as he stepped through the deep snow. Bracelets adorned his wrists, and he had a ring on each finger. His skin was smooth and dark, a contrast to his white hair. The cold didn't seem to bother him, even though he wore a thin robe.

He hummed as we traversed through the forest; it was a pleasant and upbeat tune.

Although the shaman didn't set off any alarm bells once he introduced himself, I couldn't shake the strange sensation I'd felt when he was outside in the snow staring in at us; I was ready to fight whoever was there.

We didn't have any other options available to us and getting back home seemed impossible with this snow. We had to follow him. Although things felt fine, I'd remain on high alert, he was still a stranger.

A village tucked away in the forest reminded me of the sabertooth clan hiding in the forest near Krystal Creek. They'd been there for about two years before someone discovered them. I wondered how long the shaman and his tribe had been here and nobody knew about them. *Until now.*

We walked for about ten minutes when we neared a wall of dark leaves with rocks on each side. The creepy-like plant hung like a curtain. Aziir parted the leafy-vines and allowed Penn to walk through first and then me.

"Continue straight," Aziir said behind me. "And excuse my tribe, they're not used to having visitors," he said gravely. I stopped and pulled on Penn's arm and she stopped beside me. "All I meant is they will fuss over you two." He chuckled, raising his palms. "Go on, they don't bite."

Feeling nervous, I followed Penn through the narrow cave-like hallway until we reached an enclosed area safe from the elements. It was other-worldly.

Penn stopped and glanced up. Her eyes large and bright.

The white cave ceiling had a few holes where sunlight and snow snuck through; sunlight reflected off the white walls, casting the village in enough light that they could see without fire. The snow rained down, watering the grass at our feet.

"Wow," Penn said, her eyes darting everywhere as she took it all in. "This place is surreal."

I was equally as enamored by the place as Penn was. "How is this possible?" I asked. We were in parts of the forest I never noticed before. Unless we were inside a mountain, yet we entered nowhere near one.

"Come," Aziir said, pulling us out of our trance. "Let's get you fed and clothed." He eyed Penn, who huddled into my wet jacket. "That won't do," he said, snapping his fingers.

Two women appeared from behind a curtain of darkness with bright, friendly faces and cooed over Penn, whisking her away. I wondered from which direction they'd come from and surmised they'd been standing there all along, waiting.

Although Aziir was being hospitable, I didn't want Penn out of my sights. It was my fault we got caught in the blizzard and she was my responsibility now.

"Wait—"

"Don't worry, she's in excellent hands." Aziir grabbed my forearm and pulled me in the opposite direction.

"But—"

Penn glanced over her shoulder at me. Her smile broadening as the two women fussed over her. They laughed at some joke, and I tried to relax.

"It's okay," Aziir said, grabbing my neck possessively. "She'll feel better once she's had a warm bath and has dry clothing on." He pointed up ahead. "This is you, my friend," he grinned as we neared a teepee hut with steam emitting out of the top. "You could do with a warm bath and clean clothing, too." He opened the material door and pointed once more. "Once you're done, we'll leave clothing on the stone. Now relax, make yourself at home, and enjoy."

I opened my mouth to protest but Aziir hurried toward approaching people who all wore gracious smiles; their eyes darting between me and their leader.

I stared at the hut they'd taken Penn to, but she was already inside. I exhaled a nervous breathe and reluctantly entered the teepee, and the warm air knocked the breath out of my lungs. I immediately started sweating. My eyes flitted around the circular room, but my attention went straight to the center of the hut, to the natural hot bath surrounded by large black rocks.

Hot water bubbled to the surface with steam surrounding it and the room. The air was moist yet comfortable and I sighed with relief. We were warm, and soon clean and in warm clothing. I knew I should be on high alert, but I also needed to rest.

I undressed and stepped into the shallow pool. The water was pleasant enough that I didn't feel as though I'd overheat. I used the liquid soap to wash my body and shampoo for my hair and beard. I sank down to the bottom of the hot pool and rinsed.

It was pleasant sitting in the water, but if I stayed, it would weaken my muscles to the point I could no longer defend myself in a fight.

I climbed out, used the light blue towel to dry myself, and dressed in clothing that had mysteriously appeared while I washed. Yet I heard no one. The light gray linen trousers and top fit perfectly. I pulled on the sandals and stepped out of the teepee.

Sunlight still reflected off the white walls and I guessed

it was late afternoon, early evening. A fine mist rained down, but not enough to dampen my clothing.

I headed in the crowd's direction; they circled a bonfire where some danced and sang while others stood around rectangular tables filled with food and ate.

I saw Penn before anyone realized I was nearby. She sat between the same two women who led her away earlier. They'd clothed her in a similar outfit as mine and everyone else, her hair was still damp, and her cheeks were rosy from the drink she sipped. When she glanced up at me, her smile warmed me to my toes.

"Flynn," Aziir said, grabbing my neck possessively once again. "How did you enjoy the bath?"

"It was great, thanks. And thank you for the clothing," I said, pulling on the shirt and moving away from him.

"Pleasure. Now come, eat, drink and dance." He let me go and called after one of his people.

I approached the table with food and picked up a place; out of the corner of my eye, I noticed Penn stand and head in my direction.

"They're nice," Penn said, grabbing a place. "And the food is delicious. This is my second plate already." Her grin split her face in two. "I don't know what that is," — she pointed at a dish that reminded me of pumpkin fritters, — "but they're the best." She helped herself to a spoonful of the stuff. "Come sit with us," she said, and went back to her seat between the two women.

Not wanting to be rude, I tried all the dishes and agreed with Penn. The pumpkin fritter type dish was my favorite too.

"Something to drink?" A man asked, holding a jug and empty mug.

"Sure," I said, holding out my hand. "What is this?" I

asked, sniffing the liquid inside when he handed me the mug.

"Just juice we make with the wild berries growing here. We mix it with the spring water. I'm Jake," he said, holding out his hand.

I placed the empty plate on the table and shook his hand. "Flynn," I said with a mouthful.

"Are you two from town?"

I nodded and swallowed. "Yes, we got snowed in and stuck in a cave."

"Ah," Jake said, "Aziir has a good nose for those in trouble, and it's a good thing, too. The blizzard knocked down power lines for the town and nobody can travel in or out. I doubt even snow leopards could travel in this weather."

His words did not comfort me, but it relieved me we were dry and safe.

"Anyway, welcome to our home. Shout if you need anything," Jake smiled, and one side of his cheek caved in. He kept that side of his face away from me and in the shadows; I couldn't tell if it was an old scar or a deep dimple in his cheek. "Here, let me fill that for you."

Before I could say 'no', he filled my mug again. I mumbled 'thanks' as he walked away but didn't hear me.

I glanced around for a place to sit but most of the seats were occupied. I found a vacant place opposite Penn and near the back. There were open seats near the front, but I didn't feel like mingling with strangers or being too close to the scorching flames.

Once seated, the heat from the fire beat against my chest. The chatter from the folks beside me blended with the night sounds. While the fire raged angrily in the pit, each flame licked the air as if trying to escape.

I pulled on my shirt collar. Sweat dripped down my back

and my muscles in my calves spasmed. I sipped on the juice, quenching my thirst, and rubbed my aching leg muscles.

Penn laughed at the woman's joke, then all three stared at me. Their eyes grew larger and darkened, then the edges of Penn's face warped and blurred.

My eyes flitted to the women on either side of Penn. Their faces flashed from normal to demonic and back again. I flinched, pushing the seat back, but it caught on the moist ground and fell backward. I spilled my drink, rolled off the chair, and stood up before I crashed to the ground.

Nobody seemed to care that I'd almost fallen, or that I'd broken the chair leg. Everybody carried on singing and dancing as if I wasn't there.

I needed fresh air and hurried away from the heat of the crowd and fire. The farther away I was from them, the better I felt.

When I reached the edges of the darkness where the fire barely illuminated, I sucked in cool air. Nighttime had spread throughout the cave and it had felt like only an hour since we'd arrived. I exhaled and turned back toward the crowd and froze. There was nobody sitting near the now dead bonfire and the skeletal remains of humans covered the ashen ground.

I flinched when someone grabbed my shoulder, forcing me to knock their hand off of me, spilling my drink again and falling to one side. The person grabbed me, stopping me from crashing to the ground.

"Easy there," he said gravely. "I'm not like them. I won't hurt you."

"What do you mean?" I said groggily, shaking the dizziness away, but it didn't help. I stood on shaky legs, narrowing my eyes at the stranger, but he was blurry around the edges, yet his dark eyes were unmistakably clear.

"If you want to live, only drink water you collect from the spring yourself. Don't trust what they tell you, and don't mention you met me." And as quickly as he appeared, he was gone again.

I stood dumbstruck and dizzy. Heat rose to my throat, my stomach lurched, and I fell to my knees, puking.

Chapter Nine

My stomach ached. My head was about to explode, and I couldn't remember anything after puking.

Slowly, carefully, I sat up. Before my vision tunneled, I caught glimpses of the wooden bedroom; it was tasteful and comforting. After a moment, I had to lie back down again.

"Take it easy," someone with a sultry voice said nearby; followed by a cold cloth on my forehead. "How does that feel?"

I swallowed, but my mouth was too dry. I tried speaking, but it felt as though my throat was sandpaper. After the third time swallowing, I found my voice. "Thanks." I swallowed again. "Water." Visions of a man bathed in darkness came to mind, and I quickly added. "Fresh water." I tried sitting up, but she held me down.

"I'll give you water but stay down or you'll make yourself sick again." A chair scraped across the wooden floor, then the sounds of water pouring into a mug.

I opened my eyes and turned my head in her direction,

watching her approach. "You have a sip first." I didn't trust what was in that jug.

"We didn't poison you, Flynn. Our juice purifies you of the toxins in your body, and judging from all that you expelled, you need to drink the juice again tonight."

Slowly, I sat up and it didn't feel like my brain was about to leak out of my ears. I took the mug from her and sniffed. I sipped slowly and enjoyed the fresh water; there was no strange aftertaste either.

"Our juice is a natural remedy. I assure you there is no poison. Everybody drinks it once a month, followed by two days of cleansing." The woman smiled kindly, and I wanted to trust her. She had platinum hair braided behind her back, reminding me of my mother when she was alive. The silver hair was a stark contrast to her dark eyebrows and light brown colored eyes with crow's feet when she smiled. She was… freshly baked cookies, hot cocoa on cold, rainy days. She was… home. I wanted to trust her…

But I remembered last night and what that man had said; that I shouldn't trust any of them. I wondered whether I could trust him. My head hurt from thinking.

"My name is Ally," she said, pulling me out of my thoughts, and I enjoyed another sip of the cool liquid. "I joined this tribe when I was twenty-two. I'm ninety-six now."

I choked on the water, wetting my chest and unable to breathe. After coughing, I sucked in a deep breath and found my voice. "Are you serious?"

"Yes." Ally stood and fetched something from the table and came back. "Eat. The fruit will ease the queasy feeling." She set the plate on the bed beside me. "Finish that and I'll give you more water. You're dehydrated, so drink up."

"The woman I was with. Where is she? Is she okay?"

"She's fine. She, too, wasn't feeling well and is currently resting. I'm sure by this afternoon you'll be able to see each other."

I chewed on a piece of apple, and it eased the nausea.

Ally filled my mug with water and watched me eat and drink. After I ate the apple, she gave me pieces of dried meat. When I was feeling better, exhaustion took over, and I slept.

I awoke hours later, but it felt like days. I felt disorientated. My body was stiff from sleeping in one position, and the nausea was gone.

I rolled onto my side and saw Ally sitting in the only chair in the room, reading a book. She must've felt me staring and looked up from her book. She smiled and placed her book on the table.

"Penn is awake and outside if you're up to joining her?" Ally said, removing the covers from me. "Do you feel better?"

"Much, thank you."

"Before you leave, can I ask you something?" When I nodded, she asked, "Who told you it was poison?"

I opened my mouth to say I didn't know his name when she raised her hand. I closed my mouth again, waiting.

"There's only one person who constantly complains about the tribe and he's done everything in his power to drive us apart. And with you two here, it's given him something to work against us." She folded the blanket and placed it neatly on the bed. "If he approaches you again, tell Aziir, he'll know how to manage him." Ally opened the door and ushered me outside before I could respond.

The more I thought about it, the more I realized I shouldn't respond. Whoever this person was and whatever his issue with the tribe was, was none of my business. My priority was keeping Penn and myself safe and hoped we were gone before he picked a fight with them.

Another day had passed and we were nowhere near going home. There was mist inside the cave as the blizzard continued outside. I hoped everyone in Sterling Meadow was okay and that Léon's warehouse was safe, but Jude, Lee, and Kai would cover my shift.

Unfortunately, this was our current situation. I needed to find a way out of this village and hike back to Sterling Meadow or stay here and hoped they didn't poison us.

I exhaled a frustrated breath and surveyed the village; on one side they were gardening, some were doing the washing near a water-well, while others prepared a meal in an outdoor kitchen.

My basic observation of the village was they didn't have radios, cellphones or electricity. I saw no weapons. And they lived off the land and what they had got the job done.

I put on a smile as I approached Penn, but then I stopped. She looked angelic in a white linen dress and her hair in a messy bun. She crouched between the same two women and picked flowers from a garden. When they had enough flowers, they started making flower crowns.

I didn't want to disturb the women; Penn was safe. The intricacies of their activity kept their focus on their hands, and I couldn't help but admire their creativity. And it pleased me watching Penn interact with the women. I hadn't known her for long, but she seemed content, even happy.

"Enchanting, isn't she?" said a familiar voice.

I glanced over my shoulder at Aziir, who wore a smirk and sporting round glasses with no lenses.

"Who are you referring to?"

"Penn, of course." Aziir stepped beside me. "Meredith and Elizabeth are wonderful, but Penn is special. Penn has a natural beauty to her, yet she smiles to hide her heart. And there's something else too…"

A shudder ran through me at Aziir's words and that he was watching Penn. Therefore, it wasn't the right time to ask about the juice and us falling ill. I needed to get to know him a little better, for him to trust me, and to assess whether we were in any danger. For now, I'd wait and see what happened.

"What I can't figure out is which shifter she is? You're a mighty lion. Are you not?" His smile reached his eyes. But there was something behind that dark demeanor I didn't like. When he glanced at Penn again, his smile faded.

"I am," I mumbled, not liking where this conversation was going.

"Do you know what she is?" Aziir turned toward me again, his expression void of emotion. It was unnerving how he stared directly at me, into my soul; like he was about to scoop out my brains and eat it.

"Komodo dragon," I said reluctantly. He was bound to find out, eventually. If I lied to him, he'd become suspicious, and if something sinister was going on, I needed to figure it out without drawing suspicion.

"Komodo dragon!" I flinched at his sharp, crisp words. "Well, well, well, I'd never met one before," he said, wiping the corners of his mouth. "I guess there's a first for everything." He was quiet for a moment, then added, "She doesn't enjoy shifting into her beast, does she?"

I frowned. "No." It wasn't my place to tell anyone her

43

story. If they wanted to know what had happened, they could ask her.

"Huh," he added, placing his hands behind his back and raised his head, his eyes still on Penn.

The silence stretched. I stepped away from Aziir.

My lion-beast growled inside my head, needing to get as far away from him as possible. But there was nowhere to run, and I didn't want to cause Penn unnecessary stress if I were wrong or put her in danger. For now, I would observe.

We stood in silence, watching the women for ten long minutes. The women made a flower crown each, stacking them neatly together.

I felt like a pervert gawking at them, but it wasn't only me. They had attracted a crowd; the entire village was watching.

Other women joined in to help and soon there were easily twenty flower crowns.

Someone started another bonfire, and the heat beat against my left-hand side.

A chill swept across my back, and I slowly turned around. I narrowed my eyes at the dark figure standing at the darkest part of the cave; the man from last night.

My mouth parted to call after him when he slowly shook his head and pressed his index finger to his lips. My eyes flitted to Aziir who sensed something and glanced nervously my way then at the back of the cave; where the man was standing moments ago.

Aziir called someone over and whispered in his ear. The man ran toward the dark part of the cave and he, too, disappeared.

"What's going on? Who is that man?" I thumbed behind me.

"Don't mind him," Aziir said, squeezing my upper arm.

"He's disturbed." With those parting words, Aziir made a beeline to his hut.

Someone started playing a homemade guitar and another a tambourine.

Others arrived holding plates filled with food, setting the large table.

I approached Penn, pulling gently on her arm.

"Hey, Flynn," Penn said, standing and hugging me.

She felt soft against my hard body, and I pressed my nose near her neck; she smelled of florals and vanilla.

"Are you okay?"

"I'm fine. Last night I felt sick but I'm okay now. How are you?" Her smile reached her kind eyes.

I swallowed hard. I didn't want to tell Penn my thoughts on the village for fear of scaring her. But she needed to know.

When I didn't respond quick enough, Penn cupped my face. She moved my head so that I looked her in the eyes.

"What's going on? You're scaring me?"

I grabbed her hand and walked swiftly to a private corner where no prying ears could hear us.

"There's something strange going on with this place. A man warned me not to trust the villagers." I pointed in the direction of where I'd spoken to him last night. "That they are poisoning us with that juice. The woman who helped me this morning said it was a detox. And although I feel fine now, I can't help but feel weary. Unfortunately, we have to wait for the blizzard to clear before we can leave."

Penn stared at me like I'd lost my mind. "I sense nothing," she said, glancing at the village behind me. "Maybe the juice made you paranoid? There was a hallucinogenic in it, but no lasting effects. We can trust them."

Penn rubbed my upper arms, trying to soothe me, and I

couldn't help but admire this woman. But something was off. And the next time I spoke with Penn about it, I needed proof. For now, I'd play along and not cause trouble.

"Now, I'm starving. Let's go get something to eat." Penn grabbed my hand and led me to the food table.

As I waited my turn in line, I glanced at the dark area at the back of the cave and saw four men carrying someone.

Chapter Ten

After dinner, the festivities began. At least I knew what to expect this time around.

I sat beside Penn while her keepers sat on her other side. Every time one woman spoke with Penn, anger filled my veins. I didn't want them speaking to Penn. But until I had proof detailing their strange behavior and why, I would remain quiet.

I hoped the blizzard ended soon so that we could leave. Then I'd chat to my leader Troy and Léon; they needed to be aware of this tribe.

Someone caught my eye. Jake started on one end of the large circle, pouring juice for everybody. I watched him pour the juice, and the villagers drank it. There wasn't a second jug. We all drank from the same source. Everybody was being poisoned, or medicated.

When he stopped near us, I graciously declined.

"I insist," Jake demanded, handing me the juice filled mug. The expression he wore was a stern warning. When I didn't take the mug, he bent down with his face near mine.

"You don't have to drink, just hold the mug. Let them see you're part of them or you'll only cause trouble for yourself." He glanced in Penn's direction. "And her," he whispered.

Jake stood tall once more and handed me the mug. This time I took it, nervously surveying the area, but nobody was watching. Until my eyes found Aziir, who nodded his approval. Then with his free hand he cupped an imaginary mug and brought it to his lips, mimicking drinking.

I brought the mug to my lips and tipped the mug and only allowed the liquid to touch my lips without drinking it. Then I raised the mug in celebration and faked a smile, licking my lips.

Aziir nodded his approval again and disappeared.

A hollow knot sat in the pit of my stomach and twisted. Sweat peppered my forehead and the linen clothing stuck to my skin.

I leaned against Penn and whispered near her ear that she had to pretend to drink the juice.

She kissed my cheek, smiled, and continued speaking to the two women, keeping her mug of juice on the ground.

Not wanting to leave Penn on her own, I remained seated, pretending to drink the cool-aid.

My beast growled inside my head; he wanted out and to hunt.

Penn grabbed my hand, shushing me.

The person sitting on my other side scoffed and scooted farther away, glaring daggers in my direction as he spoke to someone behind him.

I inhaled deeply, trying to calm my beast before we attracted more attention, and certainly not from Aziir.

The two women kept Penn occupied, and I couldn't help think it was on purpose; possibly alienating me or I

48

conjured everything inside my head. I stared down at the mug in my hands, at the red berry mix sloshing inside.

The fire raged before me, heating my front. On any other night, this would be an ideal evening. We could celebrate something with the leopards or the lions, and then hunt afterwards. Or an evening with Leon's vampires at a club; although they didn't like fire, they hired a Pyro technician occasionally to put on a grand display while the vampires hid behind protective shields.

Not tonight. Tonight would be like last night. Feast, drink, get ill. In that order. But I won't drink this again; I thought as I stared at the liquid once more.

I glanced up. There was a row of people behind me and the raging fire beating against my front, leaving me sweating. The clothing stuck to my armpits, my airway constricting, and I yanked my shirt down to allow cool air to caress my chest.

When the heat became unbearable, I stood up, spilled the juice, and apologized when Penn and the two women looked at me suspiciously. I dropped the mug and pushed my way through the second row of seated bodies. The indistinct murmurs died down and everybody stared at me.

I could breathe when I stepped away from the crowd. The air cooled my skin, and the fine mist a welcome relief against my hot body.

"I told you not to trust them," said the familiar voice behind me.

I spun around, coming face-to-face with him; his bloody nose was crooked. Someone had punched his eyes almost swollen shut, and his left arm was in a sling with puffy fingers sticking out of the bandage.

"What did they do to you?" I asked, my eyes flitting over his injuries.

"You need to take your pretty lady friend and leave… tonight—"

"We can't. There's a blizzard outside."

He shook his head. "I'd rather face the blizzard than those people." He jerked his chin in the crowd's direction.

"Why don't you leave if you hate it here so much?"

He stared at me like I hit him in the face. I doubted he ever considered that.

"I can never leave. None of us can. But it's not too late for you."

Footsteps sounded behind me. When I glanced over my shoulder, they were gone. I turned back, and he had left too. Whoever had been walking toward us had left in a hurry.

When I glanced at the women dancing around the fire, a nervous shiver ran through my body. Penn was dancing with them, and they all wore the flower crowns.

Penn laughed as she held the same two women's hands. The trio snaked around the fire pit in time with the music playing. The men moved the chairs farther back giving them space to dance and stood behind them, cheering the women on.

More ladies joined the three women, and they all looked ethereal in the firelight. The soft guitar music in the background complimented the laughter filling the air.

Their dance movements were slow yet coordinated, and Penn seemed to fit in just perfectly; like she'd been practicing with them for years.

As Penn danced, her eyes brightened, and her smile widened; she was elated. I liked seeing her happy especially after everything she'd been through. I wanted nothing but happiness for her. But not here, not with these people.

The men circled them, staring hungrily as they spoke

among themselves. I couldn't hear what was being said, but their hushed tones left me on edge.

The dancing stopped when the music did. Some women fell to the ground laughing, others held onto the person beside them, keeping each other up.

Penn glanced around nervously. Panic flashed on her face as she searched. For me. I stepped into the light, but the heat continued beating against me.

The two women latched onto her like a leach, and I wanted to yell at them to leave her alone, but I couldn't get closer with the fire blazing hot.

When Penn saw me, her smile reached her eyes. Her cheeks flushed and her skin glowed. She was positively radiant in the dim light.

Penn said something to the women. Both turned and glared daggers at me. I didn't know what they said, but they were unhappy. Penn approached me, leaving them.

"That was fun," Penn said, closing the gap. "Here," she said, handing me a mug. "It's expelling the toxins infecting my body. It will do the same for you. Take a sip."

"Don't drink it, Penn. It's poisonous." I glanced around, ensuring nobody heard. Luckily, everyone was too far away.

"It's not like that, Flynn," she said. The lines between her eyes deepening. "Don't you feel better after last night? I sure do." She sipped from her mug. I wanted to swipe it out of her hands and spill the contents. "I haven't felt great in a long time. These people have done nothing but welcome us with open arms. They've fed us, clothed us, the least we could do is show our appreciation." Her voice raised, causing others to turn in our direction.

A flurry of emotions struck me then. Penn was happy here; in the short time I had known her, I'd never seen her smile so much. And if I had to be honest with myself, the fruit juice made me feel better after making me ill. But...

I glanced at the darkness where he stood. Perhaps the strange man was crazy.

"Now drink. Meredith and Elizabeth assured me that after tonight, everything will be different. By drinking their juice, we connect with their tribe, the ground beneath our feet, and the heavens above us," Penn beamed. "And I'll finally feel like I belong somewhere. My calling is to live here."

"Penn, I don't know what they've done to you, but this is not your home. Your place is with your sister in Sterling Meadow." I reached for her arm, but she pulled out of my grasp.

"No, Flynn, I don't belong there. I've been nothing but a burden to her. For an entire year, she kept me from disappearing into my beast. For a year, I was nothing but an animal. I want to live where I feel completely alive. And that's here. Don't you see, Flynn. Me following you and Aziir finding us was fate." She closed the gap and fisted my shirt. "Stay with me." Her words were delicate and filled with need. Her vulnerability made my head spin. "Live with me. Here."

I didn't want to stay here. My home was at the warehouse with my brothers. But I felt a duty to stay with Penn, to keep her safe. Or at least until we got out of here.

"Now drink," she said, pushing the mug to my lips. "And finish all of it." She slurred her words, the juice taking hold of her. "They're watching us," Penn said, but her lips didn't move.

I cocked my head to the side, confused.

She tilted the mug. I opened my mouth and welcomed the cool liquid.

Water.
When she winked, I smiled.

Chapter Eleven

I was ten. I was running. My feet were bleeding. There were cuts and bruises on my body. My lion beast within roared. He roared louder the farther I ran. My home was demolished. My people slaughtered.

Dead bodies littered the ground like rubbish. Our huts were on fire; some had already crumbled to the ground, nothing but ash.

My father was nowhere to be seen and our leader sat against his hut with a knife sticking out of his chest; his eyes unseeing.

I found Mom, but she's injured.

"Run, Flynn. Get far away from here. And don't tell them where you're from," she said, pulling me into an embrace. Her body was warm and wet with her blood. I wanted to scream. "Don't tell them who you are."

I wanted to stay with her. I needed to protect her. I was her little lion.

"Flynn," Mom said, kissing the top of my head and reaching for my little hands. My hands were so much smaller in hers. My fingers were sticky and dark red. "Get away from these people. They will only cause you harm."

I glanced up at her. Her usual bright-colored blue eyes were a dull gray and full of sadness.

"I can't leave you again," I said, choking on my words.

Mom let me go, stepped away, and yelled. "Run!"

Chapter Twelve

I awoke with a jolt, falling out of bed and crashing onto the hard wooden floor. My head throbbed, my body ached, and my tongue stuck to my palate.

"Take it easy, Flynn," Ally said, grabbing hold of me under my arms and helping me stand. "That was some nightmare. Who were you fighting?"

I sat on the bed, my limbs shaky and numb; confusion set in and I rubbed my eyes. What happened last night? I was drinking water… then… Penn smiled… we were on the same page about the village… then… nothing.

"What are you thinking?" Ally handed me a glass of water.

"Thanks," I said, taking the glass and sniffing.

"Again? We do not poison guests, Flynn. I promise you—"

"How can I believe you, Ally? It's happened twice in a row. I fall into a coma until the next morning with no recollection of events of the night before. What are you doing to me and how can I ever believe what anyone says?"

Ally pursed her lips and shook her head. "I don't know what to say. Honestly, the juice we offer cleanses us of toxins. Nothing more, nothing less." She picked up the plate from the table and offered me fruit and dried meat.

"Thanks," I said, staring at the food, and a thought crossed my mind. "Last night I drank no juice. That tells me they laced your food with something similar to what's in your juice?" I set the plate onto the bed, not hungry.

"Nobody is poisoning you." Anger rolled off Ally in waves. "Your body was holding onto toxins that's detrimental to your health. You're a mighty lion shifter. You can't grow into your full potential if your body is full of poisons."

"Exactly, Ally. I'm a shifter. Not much affects me but whatever you are using knocks me out quickly and for hours. That's potent *juice*."

We stared at each other for a heartbeat; neither of us wanting to look away first.

I blinked, shaking my head. "I hope you're right." Not wanting to feel inferior to her, I stood, towering above her. "Because if you're lying to me, you will get to meet my beast first. Understood." I growled the last word.

Ally stepped away from me and lowered her head, averting her eyes.

I stormed out of the hut and the bright morning sun cascaded off the white cave walls, momentarily blinding me. A shiver ran down my back from the warmth.

When I could see again, I glanced around. It seemed like a normal day. The flower crowns worn yesterday were once again placed near the water well. And there were villagers gardening, some cooking, while others washed clothing.

There was something missing. In a village this size I'd

expect to see them but I hadn't. Not. One. Child. Some villagers were of childbearing age, yet none had.

With that in mind, it was possible I may have missed something else. I focused on my surroundings with my lion eyes and focused.

There, against their prayer hut wall, was a mural I hadn't noticed either. The painting depicted various disturbing scenes; skeletons dancing while crows circled, villagers gardening black organs, a wedding with angel wings in the sky, and lastly a party—people dressed in white dancing, wearing flower crowns with skeletons playing instruments. In the lower right-hand corner was a small animal I couldn't quite make out. It seemed out of place with the rest of the drawings, but then again, everything about it was strange.

I swallowed hard. The small animal reminded me of a cat, or a kitten. The animal had red markings. Everything about the mural left me uncomfortable. Everything within me screamed that we had to leave.

"Flynn!" Aziir slapped his hand on my shoulder and possessively kept it there. "You're looking much better today. How are you feeling?"

"Fine," I said, twisting my body out of his grasp and stepping away from him. I wanted to ask him about the juice but decided against it. I needed to first find Penn before stirring trouble. "Where's Penn?" My tone was sharp.

"She's with Elizabeth," he said, pointing at a hut I hadn't noticed before either. I frowned. There were many things I didn't see until now.

"I wanted to ask you about John." When Aziir saw me frown harder, he added, "He's the one warning you against us. The juice will cleanse your body only. I harm no one in my tribe. I only want what's best for everyone. And that's why I need to speak with you. I want you and Penn to stay."

I arched my eyebrows. I did not want to stay, but I couldn't say this until I had a plan in place, and I knew where Penn was.

"Let me chat to Penn and I'll let you know."

"Good," he said, grinning. "Don't go far. I have a surprise for you." Before I could ask what kind of surprise, he jogged to meet someone.

I approached the hut Aziir had pointed at. When I pushed the door open, I paused in the doorjamb; two naked women sat in the middle of the room with an open book between them. Their hands were on each other's shoulders, and they rocked, chanting unintelligibly.

The atmosphere in the room seemed to shift as their chanting continued, my presence unbeknownst to them.

The room was bare apart from the brightly colored murals on the wall, similar to the one I'd seen outside.

I was about to leave when something caught my eye. In the far, dark corner sat someone. They moved, casting their hair in the soft light; I recognized her hair.

Slowly, I closed the door behind me without making a noise and walked toward Penn, who sat naked in the corner. She had her legs crossed beneath her, rocking on the cold wooden floor with her arms across her chest. She mumbled words I couldn't hear; even with my lion hearing.

It worried me what they'd done to her.

I reached for her, touching her shoulder gently.

She flinched, stopped rocking, but continued mumbling as she stared out at nothing.

I crouched behind her. "Penn?" I whispered near her ear. "Are you okay?"

I wanted to pull her toward me, to pick her up and get

her out of here, but I paused, frowning; on her shoulders and back were blotches. I hoped it was dirt and not bruises.

Penn turned slowly, her dark eyes sunken and unseeing. I didn't like this. A shudder ran through me, thinking what they did to her.

We had to leave. Now.

I grabbed Penn under her arms, pulling her to her feet; picked up a robe off of the floor and pulled it over her shoulders.

I wrapped my arm around her to half-carry her and we walked out of the hut. The two women continued their chanting as if we weren't there.

When we stepped outside, we made a beeline toward the hut I'd slept in. Ignoring the stares I felt on my back, we quickly entered the hut and found the extra set of clothing Ally kept there.

Once Penn was dressed, I gave her some water to drink, but she continued staring vacantly.

"Penn?" I said, lifting her chin so she could look me in the eye.

When she noticed me, she blinked. "Flynn?" she asked, confused. "What happened?" she asked, glancing around the room.

"I don't know. You were naked in their prayer hut. I brought you here to dress." My eyes flitted to the now crinkled shirt she scrunched against her chest.

"I was with the two women…" her words trailed as she thought. "They said I had to get ready for the ceremony. And then, I don't know." She chewed on her bottom lip. "They gave me something to eat—" She couldn't finish her sentence when she doubled over, crying in pain.

"What's wrong?" I reached for her, helping her sit on

the bed. I grabbed the folded blanket and covered her shaking body.

I wanted to ask her about last night, but Ally entered, interrupting my thought process.

"You can't keep her here, Flynn," Ally said, her eyes round as saucers. "Aziir isn't pleased. He meant for the two of you to remain separated."

"I don't understand. Why would he want us separated if he wanted us to stay here?"

"I'm sorry, Flynn," Ally said, her words filled with regret. "I had to lie. We all did. If we didn't..." She blinked back tears. "I should've told you to take her and leave. Oh my gods, what have I done. You should've left with her the first night; before that first sip."

"What do you mean?" I asked. My veins filled with rage, and I growled low as my beast pushed to the front. He was hungry for her flesh. I wanted to hurt Ally, to make her pay. She could've warned us. But they were all lying to us and now we were stuck. And Penn was ill.

"You need to understand one thing, Flynn. Aziir is powerful. If we had said anything to you he would've hurt us. We couldn't." Her voice breaking.

"Tell me what's going on?"

Something knocked against the door.

Ally glanced nervously over her shoulder. She dusted a tear off her cheek, her chin trembling.

Something was there.

The knot in my stomach tightened its hold on me, and a glaze covered my skin.

Beast rushed to the front, needing me to change, to protect.

Penn moaned on the bed, and curled into the fetal position. I moved to the front of the bed, protecting her.

Scratching sounded at the door; followed by sharp nails dragging down the door.

Ally paled, grabbing the knife she'd used to slice the cheese and held it out in front of her; her arm shaking. She was afraid of whatever was out there.

"Was anything you told me true?" I asked, remembering her age.

"Everything I said was true… except the juice. Only Aziir knows the true ingredients." She paused for a moment, then continued, "All I know is it keeps us here."

I swallowed hard, thinking of the repercussions if we drank any more of the stuff, and whether we would be kept here, too.

Penn stirred behind me, waking.

Something bumped against the door. The energy in the room stilled.

A calmness brushed against me and I raised my head, standing taller.

The bed creaked and Penn stood beside me.

"How are you feeling?" I whispered.

"Better," she said. Her tone relaxed, and filled with determination. When something caught my eye, I glanced down at her; her scales emerged from beneath the skin and disappeared. I suspected a defense mechanism she used when threatened.

My fangs elongated as my lion pushed to the surface. I knew my eyes shone bright yellow.

The door knob turned.

Ally stepped forward, gripping the knife handle tightly in her hands.

The door swung open and Aziir entered, mumbling something to someone behind him, and stepped inside the room. When he saw us ready to attack, he stopped dead and raised his hands.

"What's going on here?" He demanded. His eyes flashed to Ally and anger crossed his features. "I thought I told you to watch them. Not aid in their delusions." His eyes flitted to me and back to the knife in Ally's hand. "Everybody calm down. Relax!" He moved his hands in an up and downward motion as if trying to stop us from doing something.

Beast was ready to attack; to taste the vital fluid running through his deceitful veins.

"We want to leave," I demanded. "Thank you for your hospitality, but I think we should head back to town."

"It's snowing—"

"Don't care. Penn's sister is probably sick with worry. I'm sure we can make it."

Aziir blinked but remained silent.

Visions of cloaks came into my mind's eye; I blinked them away.

Aziir focused on me, standing taller. He exhaled, sounding exhausted. "As I explained earlier, the juice cleanses—"

"I have no memory for the rest of the evening. Why? One moment I was fine, the next moment it's morning."

"It's part of a cleansing ritual we do monthly. But when we have newcomers, we indulge once more. There are no side effects, and besides, I wanted you to see my village in its truest form," he said, raising his arms and slightly to the side as if something was on display. Then rested his arms at his sides. "I want you to stay here with us."

"We can't," I said, shaking my head and grabbing Penn's hand.

Aziir pursed his lips. "That's fair," — he exhaled, — "but before you go—"

I opened my mouth to say something when Aziir shushed me.

"Hear me out, Flynn, please. Before you go, I have a gift. I'm sure when we're done, the snow would let up and you're welcome to leave."

Chapter Thirteen

Penn wrapped her arm around my middle and nestled under my arm. It was an intimate gesture. This would have been the perfect date night; we could be a normal couple standing outside watching the stars and enjoying a glass of something delicious.

Instead, we huddled together, too afraid of letting the other go, and surrounded by people but trusted no-one.

I wanted to be the type of man Penn could rely on; her protector. And I knew she could be the type of woman who kept me grounded.

Unfortunately, we couldn't do anything except watch and wait for the right moment to escape.

All the villagers congregated in the open area near the fire pit. I didn't know what we were waiting for, but nobody said a word. The silence was like a sharp blade constantly slicing into my chest; death by a million paper cuts.

Penn shivered against me and I tightened my hold on her. I kissed the top of her head, reassuring her that there was hope. We weren't romantically involved, but we shared our own kind of intimacy. We shared this journey and I would do everything I could to get her safely home to her sister.

"I don't like this," Penn whispered against my chest. I felt the vibrations of her words strike my heart.

"Me neither," I said with my lips against her head. "Let's get closer to the exit. When the time comes, run as fast as you can."

She nodded, exhaling.

As one, we stepped to the side. Nobody noticed. We took another small step and stopped when movement to the side caught my attention.

Aziir strolled through the crowd. He passed the fire pit and headed for the left-hand side of the cave. There was nothing other than dirt and the white cave walls and I wondered where he was going. The nearest hut was a short distance in the opposite direction.

Aziir seemed to walk straight for the wall, but then he disappeared behind a wall of rock, reminding me of the first day we met when his translucent shoulder materialized once he allowed us to see him. The same thing happened now. It was like he dissolved into the rock.

He appeared again a few feet in the air; his body slowly emerging from the rock. We could only see him from the waist up, reminding me of someone standing behind a pulpit.

I wondered whether he blended with the shadows and listened in on conversations. It would explain why Ally was so afraid to say something before.

When Aziir raised his hand, the crowd fell deathly silent, giving him their undivided attention. I doubted anyone dared to breathe.

A quick glance around and I noted Ally and Jake stood

a short distance away from us and they, too, stood fascinated by their leader.

When Aziir spoke, I flinched, his voice was deep and authoritative. His words were an ancient language I'd never heard before, and waves of goosebumps spread across my skin, making me shiver.

Penn leaned into me and she too seemed affected by Aziir's voice or the words he spoke; I didn't know which, but they were equally powerful.

The crowd stood mesmerized by Aziir and it was in that moment I understood why he was their leader. He wore white from head to toe. His dark skin was a stark contrast to the white goatee and head full of white hair. His piercing dark blue eyes were no longer warm or welcoming; they were blazing with contempt.

"Do you know what he's saying?" I whispered, afraid to bring unwanted attention to us.

Penn nodded, glancing up at me. "Someone has betrayed their trust and needs to be punished. Then he rambles on about commitment and loyalty." She listened for a moment, then when Aziir's expression became animated, angry, she added, "Someone really pissed him off."

As Aziir spoke, his bracelets on his wrists jangled. When he pointed toward the crowd and then there was movement, we focused on the sea of bodies making a path for someone to walk through them; John.

They had tied John to a large wooden pole and carried him toward the area near Aziir, placing him on the ground. I'd expected him to untie himself, jump up and run away, but he didn't; he just lay there, unmoving. I couldn't see his chest moving, neither.

Penn turned in my embrace and buried her face into my clothing. I held her tighter against me and kissed the top of her head again. We took another step closer to the exit tunnel.

"I brought you to this village because you needed a safe place," Aziir said in English and looked in our direction. We stopped walking when all eyes turned on us. "When I found Flynn and Penn out in the cold with no food or proper shelter, I knew I had to do something. We have enough here to provide and care for them."

Some villagers moved as one, stepping closer toward us, and blocking our exit.

"I'm not the bad person here. I have hurt no one, but I have freed you of the outside world that poisoned your body. The juice we offer rids you of the toxins placed there by institutions who wish to control you. They have inserted various tracking devices and nano technology that control you over the airwaves."

I couldn't help but frown at his speech. It sounded like something from a science fiction novel.

Penn turned around in our embrace, but kept her back against my front and held onto the sides of my pants.

"What we do, as a loving community, is when required, we willingly sacrifice someone as tribute to the gods for keeping us safe in a world no longer ours. It is a world we share with greedy corporate CEOs and government institutions who do nothing but fill their pockets with money and experiment on the population like guinea pigs."

Aziir's eyes rolled into the back of his head. His skin darkened as his hair turned black. His white coat burst into flames, revealing a black cloak underneath.

"Since living here," — Aziir raised his hands in worship, — "we have weathered many storms. Losing many babies because of outside influence. But, we are stronger together, and the two newcomers might stay with us. And with them, they bring fresh blood to our village; and a new vision. May the beast within us roar loudly as he takes shape around us, comforting us."

The person beside us glanced over his shoulder at the painting on the hut. Penn followed his line of sight and gasped.

"Unfortunately, for years, none of our women have been able to conceive..."

I glanced at Ally, who averted her eyes and stared at the ground. With her left hand, she wiped her cheek.

"...so our hope lies with our new guests," Aziir said, pointing at us. "Stay," he added, and disappeared. When he materialized again, he was near the exit. "We can't allow you to leave. We need you as much as you need us. Stay." Aziir closed the gap, reaching for me.

Visions of my mother protecting me as a ten-year-old boy crashed into me. Followed by men in dark cloaks surrounding the village, surrounding us, and with it, other memories came to the front. Memories I'd long forgotten; memories I had to forget in order to move forward.

Lions. My family. My village. Men in cloaks who needed lion shifters as offering to their gods upon an eclipse of the sun. The fireball in the sky blocked out by a blood moon. And their sacrifice, was not just any kind of lion...

Me...

"My boy, you remember—"

"What do you know?" I scowled.

"Tell me, Flynn. Is it not true that your mane goes sun-soaked yellow when you change into your spectacular beast, and the outer edges are much, much darker; revealing how powerful you truly are."

I swallowed hard, narrowing eyes at him. How could he

have known anything about my beast? I hadn't changed into him since being here.

Aziil smiled sinisterly. "You were young when it happened; I doubt you remember most of it. Yes, it was an horrific event, but it had to be done. To keep my people strong and fertile we needed to sacrifice the most powerful lion." He stepped forward and almost touched me. I swatted his hand away and pulled Penn backward with me.

"Don't touch us," I yelled, curling my lips over my blunt human teeth.

"We asked your father for an offering or face destruction. Naturally, he refused. He was willing to sacrifice his entire clan just to keep you safe. His tiny lion," Aziir said sinisterly. "I didn't know how powerful you were until your father denied us. Denied me." Aziir's eyes glowed red with anger.

"Unfortunately, after we destroyed everything, we couldn't locate you. I knew you were somewhere in the village but couldn't pinpoint exactly where. I remember the day like it was yesterday." Aziir stood taller with his hands behind his back and wearing a smug expression.

I desperately wanted to bite into him and rip out his throat.

"I stood in the middle of the village with all that death and destruction and closed my eyes, praying," Aziir said. "In that quiet moment, I understood I needed to be patient. That sacrificing you then wasn't the right time. Instead, I had to wait, and have faith that you would come to us on your own.

"So we left, and we waited. We waited for the day, and it happened when you got stuck in the snow. A snowstorm we had been praying for. And you brought her with." Aziir proffered a hand at Penn, but she shook her head.

"Waiting for you has been challenging. My people have been suffering. But it was worth it." His voice changed; his tone was deeper and blood curdling. "But before we can continue with you two, we have a sacrifice that's long overdue." He turned his attention to John, who remained unconscious on the ground.

Four men headed toward the exit and stood guard while another four approached John. They picked up the wooden pole they tied him to and carried him to the fire pit. They placed him on the stone slab surrounding the pit and untied him.

Aziir approached John with menacingly purpose.

The air became stuffy as his power beat against us. He removed a blade from the cuff of his left sleeve and raised his arm.

Chapter Fourteen

My mind buzzed with the possibilities, but there was only a handful of probabilities. As a lion shifter and I could tear a human apart in seconds, but if ten men attacked with knives, I'd be dead.

And although Aziir had said they needed me, I doubted they would hesitate to kill me if they thought I was a threat to their village.

I silently cursed myself for not leaving after that first night. I should've taken Penn and ran; we could've braved the weather and be back home. But events had happened that were out of my control. Now we found ourselves in quite the predicament.

John had warned me. Multiple times he had said that I shouldn't trust them; to take Penn and run as fast as we could. I only had myself to blame for the situation we found ourselves in.

Penn turned in my embrace and stood beside me. She rounded her shoulders and her scales flashed in the light;

casting her skin in a silver, purple, and green glow, reminding me of fish scales.

When Penn glanced up at me, I realized I wasn't in this alone; I had Penn. And she was a very dangerous Komodo dragon.

Penn had previously said she didn't want to change for fear of being stuck in her beast. It was a valid concern, and I didn't blame her. But the twinkle in her eye as her second eyelid closed and opened again, I knew she would help. That as a team we could escape.

Without saying a word, we stepped away from each other.

Aziir brought his hand down and, in one swift motion, sliced John's neck; his flesh splitting open, and blood poured out of the fresh wound.

John screamed as he awoke from his induced slumber; a rude awakening as he grabbed the gaping hole in his throat, desperately trying to hold it closed.

Penn rounded her shoulders once more and jerked her chin toward our exit.

I stepped closer to the four men guarding the exit, grateful the sacrifice near the fire pit preoccupied them.

Penn didn't wait for me or bother removing her clothing. She screamed as loud as she could, ripped open the large top and leaped into the air. Her clothing shredded to strips of material.

The four men to my left realized what was happening and approached. Men on our right neared too. Soon they'd box us in.

I tore at my shirt, a button popped off, and lunged forward. When I landed on all fours, I roared as loud as I could as my beast stretched, happy to be out, and he was hungry.

I was larger than the average lion shifter and the only one with a mane that had darker edges. My eyes glowed a similar shade to the sun-soaked yellow mane and body.

I glanced to my right and Penn stood gloriously in her much larger Komodo dragon. I didn't know she was so massive. Beast and I stared in wonder; her large, thick, scaly back and toothy jaw reminded us of an ancient dinosaur forgotten by time. If she stood on her hind legs, I was sure she'd easily be eight feet; which was tall for a female.

Penn hissed at everyone around her; the warning meant danger for anyone who came near us.

The villagers screamed and scattered in various directions; avoiding Aziir and us. The eight men who wanted to attack froze, looking to the other for confirmation. I suspected they understood the depths of their demise if they did approach us.

I grinned when two men ran away.

Aziir screamed, taking his anger out on poor John, slicing his neck and back multiple times. John's blood sprayed everywhere, drenching the grass in his thick, red vital fluid.

"No!" Aziir screamed and approached us, but his attention was for Penn, who swished her huge tail backward and forward; reminding me of an agitated cat.

"Let us leave," I said through my toothy jaw. "Or we eat." I added, curling my lips over my sharp teeth.

The men to my left stepped back.

"No!" Aziir seemed conflicted. "I have prophesied that you will end my people's suffering. This isn't how it's supposed to end." He swapped the knife in his hands, moving it from his left to right hand, as he decided what to do.

Penn lost patience and charged the three men closest to her.

Using the element of surprise, I lunged for the closest man; to kill one before the other two realized what had happened. Neither attacked. When they saw their friend on the ground with his throat in pieces, they sprinted away.

Penn stood with a severed arm in her mouth, the rest of him beneath her sharp claws. The other two men didn't move or try to fight.

Dark blood covered the ground; it was a mixture of brown, green, and gloomy red. Flashes of my village caught me off guard and I froze. My vision tunneled and the only thing I heard was an emptiness that threatened to burst my eardrums.

Penn hissed, bringing me out of my stupor.

I blinked back tears.

Beast roared loudly.

Aziir flinched but didn't attack. We outnumbered him. His villagers had scattered away, leaving him to fend for himself. He understood he wouldn't survive if he attacked us.

Penn's hiss turned into something scarier, sinister, reminding me of a velociraptor from a movie I'd seen. She closed the gap, ready to strike Aziir.

Aziir's eyes flitted between Penn and me. He squeezed the knife handle in his hand and stepped backward.

We stepped forward so that we were only a short distance away from him. If I leaped into the air, I would land on him. Beast wanted to eat his soft insides.

The growling hiss from Penn echoed inside the large cave, causing the tips of the stalactites to break off and rain down on us.

Aziir paled, stood straight, and his shoulders dropped

ever so slightly. The knife fell to the ground with a soft clank. When he opened his eyes, they shone brightly with unshed tears. "This was not how you save my people," he whispered.

Penn didn't hesitate. She charged him. I joined her in the attack. She went for his legs; he collapsed onto the ground and tried to crawl away. While I gripped the back of his neck and bit down hard.

A strange gargling noise came from Aziir, who was unable to free himself from two sets of powerful jaws.

I punctured the skin and bit down harder until a tooth struck his spine. Aziir stilled. His death didn't take long with Penn's poison working quickly through his bloodstream, his heart pumping quicker.

When I tasted something bitter, I let go of his neck and allowed Penn the opportunity to finish him; which was quick.

Chapter Fifteen

Penn wiped dark coagulated blood from her forehead and cheek while I did the same from my shoulders and neck. Their vital fluid wasn't like blood from a human or supernatural. I didn't have time to process what caused the strangeness; we had more important things to focus on... like getting out.

Ally entered the hut I'd slept in previously and handed us clean clothing. Without saying a word, I understood what we did for the villagers. We freed them. It wasn't as Aziir had predicted, but I preferred this way.

The flicker of hope shining in Ally's eyes when she gave me a bundle of clothing spoke volumes. They were freed from the tyrant who had kept them hostage all these years, and now they had a future to look forward to.

Ally left the hut and quietly closed the door behind her. The moment the door closed, the voices outside eased, followed by words of thanks along with cries of worry.

Penn stopped washing her arm and looked at me through the mirror. "I didn't know they were so suppressed." She noted a drop of dry blood on her left temple and wiped it clean. "When their leader was alive, everybody seemed so happy and vibrant. Either he used his power over them or they are excellent actors."

"I think he fed them something to keep them docile and from turning against him. He was delusional in his thinking, keeping them under his stronghold for decades," I said, pulling on the pants. "I mean Ally doesn't look a day over forty-five, yet she's ninety-six."

Penn stopped wiping her face and gawked at me. "I wonder how old everybody else is."

I shrugged. "Exactly. I wonder how long they had to drink the juice before they stopped aging." I didn't express my worry about drinking the juice and the delayed effects it would have on us. If it was something we had to worry about I'd chat to Seraphine, one of the best witches in Sterling Meadow, for guidance.

"Do you think we've been affected?" Penn asked as if reading my mind.

"I don't know. The sooner we leave, the better. I don't want to stay here another minute."

"Do you think they can leave?"

I shrugged, considering her question. "I doubt they were the issue. It was Aziir. He was the one keeping them hostage. We can chat with Léon. Perhaps there's a place for them somewhere."

She smiled sadly and continued dressing in silence.

I did the same. I doubted Penn was in the mood for idle chit-chat.

Much had happened the last three days and I was grateful Penn and I had survived. It surprised me Penn had shifted into her Komodo dragon but if it wasn't for her, we might not have made it. She exuded the type of strength I wanted in a partner, and whether anything would happen between us, I was content just being friends.

Once clothed, we exited the hut. Outside stood every villager, waiting with hopeful expressions.

Jake and Ally approached us first, each holding a basket filled with food.

"What's going on?" I asked as I took the basket out of Ally's hands.

"We cannot go with you," Ally said, glancing at the exit tunnel. "We cannot leave, but you must hurry."

"I don't understand."

"We've been drinking the juice for too many years and the damage cannot be reversed," Jake said, handing Penn a basket. "Our village is protected by his magic, and with Aziir gone, we don't know how long we will survive—"

"Come with us."

"We can't," Ally said, shaking her head. "We haven't left the village since *that* day."

"What do you mean?" My brows knitted together, and I folded my arms, keeping the basket handle in my right hand.

"We were there that day," Jake said solemnly. "Aziir forced us to attack your village, Flynn. We didn't understand why, only that it had to be done, and there was no way we could stop him if we tried. When he couldn't locate you, he brought us here, protecting the cave. He was the only one allowed to leave. If any of us tried to leave, we perished before we reached the end of the tunnel."

"We know witches who can help—"

Jake held up his palm. "You don't understand. Your people fought hard that day. No one survived except you and Aziir."

Jake stepped closer and raised his arm, turning his hand

palm side up. Then, with his other hand, he pulled out a sharp blade and sliced his palm. The gaping wound had no blood.

Penn gasped when the wound knitted together.

"I don't understand," I asked. "How was John able to bleed? And the men we killed?"

"Aziir's power gave us bodies that needed air, food, and could bleed. And only Aziir could free us," Ally said. "He bound us to the cave, trapping our spirit with a body that never aged. It was only he who could free us." She swallowed hard. "We begged him to let us go. But no matter what we told him, his delusions got worse. Whether it was the government injecting us with nano bots or something else," — Ally shook her head, — "anyway, every day was a different thing. But he always thought you were the one who could save us. To rescue us from our fate. But it was Aziir all along."

"That's why John couldn't leave," I said. "The reason he warned us to get out."

Ally nodded. "We feared Aziir. If we said anything to you, he would hurt you and turn you into one of us. We couldn't allow another innocent to become his victim. We made our own choices by following him, willingly, but we couldn't allow you to fall in the same fate unknowingly." Ally fell silent for a moment. Her expression filled with a flurry of emotions; anger, shame, hurt, sorrow. "Please forgive us."

"It's not your fault," Penn said, rubbing Ally's arm reassuringly. "What happened to you is Aziir's fault." Penn bit her lower lip. "I wonder if something can be done."

"We've tried before, and it didn't work. And with Aziir gone, nobody knows how long we'll remain in this state."

"When we get back home, we'll find a way. We have witches who may know something."

Dressed warmly, Penn and I headed for the exit tunnel. I glanced over my shoulder and noted the crowd had dispersed. What Aziir did to his people was cruel. It explained why none had children and why Aziir wanted me and Penn to procreate. I'd miss the sounds of children laughing if I was in their position.

Aziir had cursed his people after they died and then kept them here. It was a cruel punishment, one no one but Aziir should've endured.

It amazed me we could destroy Aziir so easily. I kept waiting for him to come back from the dead like a bad horror movie, but he didn't. The villagers made sure of that and burned his remains, the fire still ablaze.

I knew Aziir's power was potent, but never imagined it to be so ghastly. And to think he thought I could somehow release his people from their demise was insane. There was no way I could do that.

It was all too much to comprehend. I wanted to get home and see what we could do to set everyone free. Whether it was just their spirits that needed cleansing or if a spell was needed to be broken. Someone had to help.

Chapter Sixteen

Penn and I followed the tunnel out but instead of seeing snow on the other side, the warm sun greeted us, and the forest was its lovely shade of green.

It confused me. We were only at the village for a couple of days, and I saw it snowing outside, yet what I saw suggested we may have been gone for much longer. But it didn't explain the snow I'd seen.

We circled the area and eventually found a used path. We followed it to the river and then to the edge of the forest.

The moment we saw tall buildings, and heard the sound of traffic, Penn started crying. Tears welled in my eyes as relief crashed into me at once. A flurry of emotions struck, but it relieved me we were almost home.

We started running, block after block, until we reached the warehouse. I banged on the door so hard it dented. Lee opened, mumbling absurdities for the intrusion. When he saw it was us, he pulled me in for a bear hug and didn't let go until Kai tore us apart.

Everybody spoke at once; I didn't understand a word.

"What happened?" Kai finally asked above the noise of questions. "And where have you been? We tore the forest and town apart, looking for you two. The video footage we found showed you entering the forest, but your trail went cold soon after entering. It's like you two disappeared."

I told them what had happened. While Natalie held onto Penn, not letting her sister go for anything, even accompanying her to the bathroom.

It amazed everyone that we were still alive, and it confused me since they said it had only snowed for one day. It was like Penn and I were in another world or dimension.

Lee told the leader of his Leap, Sebastian, about the events and he would hold a meeting with the Were-Animal Alliance to secure a witch or five to help free the villagers; there were things they could try.

The next day, I headed the expedition back into the forest. I found the tracks that Penn and I had left, and we followed the path until we came across rocks where the tunnel entrance was supposed to be.

"I don't understand it," I mumbled, my hand on the black-faced rock. "This is the entrance to their village," I mumbled. "I'm sure of it." I glanced at our surroundings, and it was as I remembered, except for this big, black rock.

Seraphine, one of our powerful local witches, stepped forward and pressed her palms against the rock. She closed her eyes and sucked in air, holding her breath.

"The rock is warm for such a chilly day," she said, exhaling. Her eyes were still closed when she pressed her right ear against the rock. She hummed as she listened.

A witch from Seraphine's coven joined us and she, too, hummed as she pressed her left ear on the rock. The silence stretched as the two witches *listened*. I heard nothing, even with my super sensitive hearing.

"I hear them," the witch said, stepping away from the rock.

"I hear them too," Seraphine said. "Get back," she added, ushering everyone away.

There were six more witches with Jude and I. Léon couldn't spare any vampires since we were hiking during the day, and I didn't think we needed any more shifters. The villagers were harmless now that Aziir was gone.

"I sense the shaman's power. He was ancient and possibly crazy. I've never sensed anything quite like him. Are you sure you destroyed him?" Seraphine asked, the lines between her eyes deepening.

I jolted backward as if struck by an invisible fist. I watched Penn rip into him, while I tore parts of him that would never regenerate. We had destroyed Aziir.

"He's dead," I said. "We watched him burn."

"You don't sound convinced," Seraphine said with one side of her mouth curving upward. "I'm just kidding." She slapped my shoulder. "His magic binds them still, but it's fading. He is gone, but his magic won't last. Whatever we have to do must happen now. We might fail, but I'm confident we can do something."

"Are we going with the Devil's Cure incantation?" Asked the witch who had joined Seraphine near the rock.

"I think so, Cybil," Seraphine said, opening her coat and removing a box with tiny vials. "Wait before you start." Seraphine sprinkled a fine silver powder in front of the rocks, mumbling something.

Jude and I stepped back and watched the witches work.

"Is there anything else you can remember?" Jude asked, watching the witches.

"No, I've told you everything," I said, giving Jude my attention. "I remember nothing different. I thought that perhaps my beast may have picked up on slight differences, but there's nothing. It all felt real as we're standing here now."

"There was barely any snow the day you went missing. And when we headed into the forest, your scent and tracks had disappeared. It's as if something swallowed you into the ground or into the air." Jude scratched his chin. "It's bothering me."

"I still think Aziir made it snow. It was too early for a blizzard and, as you can see, it's only autumn. He set some kind of trap for me and unfortunately I brought Penn with me."

Jude shook his head. It disturbed him that they could not locate us. We were friends and work partners, and I suspected he felt guilty for what had happened.

I reached for my friend and squeezed his shoulder. "Don't beat yourself up, my friend. It's over. I just want to move forward."

He nodded curtly. "I know, but I want to look into this."

"Do what you need to, just be careful." I exhaled a frustrated breath.

The witches had been quiet on our walk through the forest, but now that they were working, they were extremely talkative. Cybil and another witch helped Seraphine sprinkle a murky green liquid on the ground near the entrance and then they stood in a semi-circle near it.

Jude and I stepped farther back, allowing them space.

The witches did their thing. They danced and stepped in unison to music only they heard. The ground beneath my feet vibrated as their power pulsed in the air and all the hairs on my body stood up.

Jude shivered beside me and stepped farther away.

I watched in awe as the rock disappeared and the same tunnel we'd used yesterday revealed itself. The witches congratulated each other and headed through the tunnel.

When Jude and I followed them through the tunnel and out the other side, I stopped dead and swallowed my breath. It felt like I was in a different world compared to yesterday.

The sunlight no longer reached the inside of the dark, murky cave. Dark ash floated near our faces and covered the ground. The huts had crumbled, and the fire pit held bright dark ash that smoked. The area where we had destroyed Aziir had dark blotches where his blood had touched, and no ash fell there.

"I don't understand." I crossed the open area and headed for the hut I slept in. Only the outer shell of the hut remained. Everything else was destroyed, burned to the ground.

The ominous cave walls moved as darkness shifted against the sides of the cave.

The witches shrieked, ready to attack with the glowing orbs in their palms. Luckily Seraphine calmed them, avoiding a war with shadows and from destroying the cave with us inside.

The shadows moved as one toward us. Jude and I stepped farther back and away from the shit-storm that was about to happen. The shadows separated until they stood on their own; each an outline of a person. I recognized Jake and Ally's shadows. Jake had a dent in his cheek when he smiled.

"You came back," Jake's shadow said, sounding far away yet close.

"I said I'd be back, and I brought help." I pointed at the witches, and stepped out of their way. "Will you allow them to do their thing?" I asked, my eyes flitting from one shadow to the next. It saddened me to see that they were lost souls stuck in a dark cave with no escape. I hoped the witches could help them.

"Thank you, Flynn," Ally's shadow voiced, and bowed her head slightly. "When Aziir said you'd save us, I didn't think that this is what he meant. But you are saving us. Thank you."

"We have to free them soon," Seraphine said gravely.

The ground beneath our feet shook and stalactites broke and fell near where we stood. If we waited any longer we'd be impaled by one.

"I don't know how long this cave can hold," Seraphine said. "And I can only guess that they'll be trapped inside when it does."

"Do your thing," I said, pushing Jude back.

The witches ushered the shadows together and formed a circle around them; it looked like they surrounded a black hole. The air snapped as their power filled the cave. Wind whipped against my skin and I was grateful I had a beard. The wind formed a tornado around the witches and shadow-souls. The witches chanting became louder as their power pushed the air out of my lungs, forcing Jude and me back a few more steps.

Seraphine said words I didn't understand, and the blackness of the shadows turned gray. The witches continued their chanting, along with Seraphine's incantation. The gray shadow-souls became lighter and lighter until there was nothing left of them but bright light.

I blinked back tears as emotions surfaced; memories of my clan being slaughtered, along with Aziir's people. The memory of hiding beneath my mother as she died saddened me, and then the thought of never seeing my father again; I didn't know where his body was so I never got to say goodbye to him.

Flashes of the blood and carnage left me nauseated. Everything was for nothing. It only brought death and destruction. It saddened me the lengths one madman had gone to for selfish reasons, and because of delusions. I wondered what had happened to him to cause such confusion and hatred.

Aziir was a powerful shaman. I shuddered to think what would've happened if he found me that day; what he would've done to me if he did.

But it didn't end that way and it relieved me the villagers were now safe and free of their gilded cage. The cave was nothing but an empty shell filled with memories of those long gone but never forgotten.

The witches finished their incantation and the bright lights rose to the tiny holes in the cave, then finally they winked out.

We stood around as darkness surrounded us. Nobody said a word as we picked up our belongings and headed for the exit.

The hike back home was somber, but at least Penn and I were safe, and all the souls were free.

Chapter Seventeen

A week had passed since the witches released the spirits to where they belonged. Penn and I still needed time to process the events, yet at the same time neither of us wanted to dwell on the past either. Therefore, we took it one day at a time.

I wiped the table clean, rinsed the cloth, and checked the area one last time. It felt like the only thing I did around here was clean the kitchen.

Penn sat at the table, keeping me company. "Want to catch another movie tonight?" She asked without looking up from the newspaper. She enjoyed a bite of her jam toast and chewed loudly.

"Only if it's an action movie and I hold the popcorn. Yesterday you finished the box." I rinsed the cloth again and placed it neatly on the side of the sink.

"Sure," she said, glancing up with a naughty grin. "I'll hold the chocolates."

I smiled. "Sure."

Every day since we'd been back, we watched a movie,

shared popcorn, chocolate, and juice. We held hands and kissed. Penn wasn't ready to go any further than that… yet.

"Perhaps we should have dinner before," Penn said, turning the page without glancing up.

That piqued my interest and I smiled. "There are a few places we can eat."

"I would like to go to the one where all the shifters hang out."

My smile reached my eyes. This restaurant was the local hangout for all were-animals. They could go there to enjoy a meal in peace or use it as a safe place to shift into their animal and hunt with others. Penn stating she wanted to go there when at first she blatantly refused made my heart sing with joy.

Considering everything Penn had gone through, I didn't want to push her into doing anything shifter related. I knew she would come around on her own and when the time was right.

I was proud of her, every day she opened herself up to more of my world and what the shifters could offer, and every day a part of me was falling madly in love with her.

She was a gentle creature beneath that very dangerous exterior, and I would show her every day that she was desired, appreciated, and wanted.

She stood up from her seat and closed the distance. I leaned against the counter and opened my arms, enveloping her.

I kissed the top of her head and whispered near her ear. "Put on those cute white sneakers I bought you and a pretty dress. Who knows, we might go dancing later."

She leaned back and looked up at me with a matching grin. "You're such a romantic."

"I try my best."

"Let's go," she said, rocking onto her toes and kissing me chastely. "I'd love to see you in that new shirt I bought you."

I groaned inwardly but continued to smile. This blue flannel shirt made me look like a cowboy, and as much as I hated the garment, I'd wear it because it made her smile.

Next in the Shifter Days, Vampire Nights, & Demons in between Series

www.vinci-books.com/jude

When hunting monsters became falling for one.

They vanished without warning. I chased their trail through a portal and into a realm of prowling blue wolves where an Egyptian goddess held dark secrets. As a were-tiger, I was usually an apex predator. Here? I was prey. Finding my friends could cost me my life—or worse, my heart.

Turn the page for a free preview…

Jude: Chapter One

Flynn and Penn vanished that one snowy day a week ago. When we searched for them, their scent and tracks had disappeared; like they never existed.

Their disappearance didn't sit well with me, along with other parts of that day felt off. It snowed when it shouldn't have. The air was stuffy during the search in the forest, along with a constant buzz of power in the atmosphere.

Being an amateur sleuth-tiger-shifter, I needed to investigate the events more closely; whenever I entered the forest near where they disappeared, I still felt the pull of that power lingering in the air. This told me that something was still there, something was keeping the power alive.

Flynn and Penn were gone for five days, only to reappear with an intriguing story to tell. The events that took place over those five days sounded horrible and filled with sinister activities.

A deranged shaman held the two captive, and he almost succeeded in keeping them as hostages in a phantom village deep within the forest in Sterling Meadow.

We were all elated they were home and unharmed, but I couldn't help shake the feeling that something else had happened. It wasn't only the shaman's power that kept the people in their ghostly village, but something otherworldly.

Something else was out there, and I would figure it out.

"I really wish you would leave it be," Flynn said, munching on a slice of toast with a thick layer of blueberry jam. He licked the corners of his mouth but missed a crumb.

"I won't be long," I said, packing a bag of nuts, the sandwich I'd made, and two liters of water into a backpack.

"Do you have your cellphone?"

"I'm not forgetful like you," I grinned, patting my jacket chest pocket where I kept my cellphone. If only Flynn had his cellphone on his person that day, we could've rescued them in time.

"Ha, you're funny," Flynn smiled; ever since he and Penn's near-death experience, they grew closer every day, and he smiled often. It almost made me smile… Almost.

"I should be back by nightfall," I said, opening the back door to the warehouse we guarded for Léon, our Master Vampire boss. "And if I'm not home, phone me. I might have fallen somewhere and need rescuing." I slapped Flynn's chest, and he almost dropped his toast.

"Don't say that," he grumbled as I closed the back door.

Jude: Chapter Two

I traversed the same path Flynn and Penn had walked that fateful day. The hairs on my arms stood up as drops of sweat slipped down my spine.

The potent power continued pulsing in the forest.

I stepped off the path and headed for an old fallen tree. Its bark was rotten with insects crawling in and around it. In the distance, I heard the trickle of a stream.

Here, I felt the cool wind against my damp clothing and felt the sun warm my face and neck. There was no power here. I glanced over my shoulder, focusing on the trees, leaves, and bushes near the path.

Time passed. The wind stopped blowing and the call of the birds silenced.

The leaves moved gently, as if invisible hands were slowly caressing them. The dark green bushes barely moved, but here, too, I caught glimpses of invisible movement; as if someone had walked past.

My thoughts drifted to a cemetery filled with damned souls unable to move freely or where they're meant to be.

Up ahead, the face of the mountain stood ominously, with deep shadows and dark crevices. The sun shone brightly behind the mountain, slowly brightening the rocks and forest floor before me.

I glanced at the worn path once more, and a shudder ran through me. Something was off. This wasn't the forest I'd frequently hiked to enjoy forest bathing; a self-prescribed therapy. No, this forest had changed.

The world moved quickly. Humans worked harder these days and for much longer hours. While their children barely had time to play as kids, and instead became addicted to whichever device was their favorite.

My job fighting evil supernaturals would take its toll on me. So, to quieten my sensitive soul, I'd come here and sit in the calm atmosphere of the trees, leaves, and mountainous shadow to ground myself. To forest bathe.

I sucked in air over my teeth, but sensed nothing out of the ordinary, and approached the path. Once I reached the path the ghostly fingertips of its power touched me as I moved through an invisible film-like bubble.

I stood on the path, closed my eyes, and inhaled deeply. Again, there was nothing different; I smelled damp sand at my feet, the fresh blossoms on a nearby tree, and heard the buzzing of bees. The wind whistled through the tree branches, but there were no other sounds.

As I exhaled, the air popped and my eyes shot open, and I focused ahead of me. Near one of the older oak trees was a sparkly black dot. I cocked my head to the side, waiting, watching, but nothing else happened; it just sparkled. I stepped closer and poked the dot with my index finger. It pulsed and grew rounder.

The sparks of the moving black circle spat at me, reminding me of fireworks that struggled to ignite. I poked it again. It exploded into a firework display and the circle became large enough for me to step through.

When I glanced over my shoulder at the path I'd taken, and then up ahead; I was the only one here. I reached for my cellphone, dialed Flynn's number and he answered on the first ring.

"What's wrong?" He breathed into my ear as if he was running.

"I found something," I said, taking a picture of the large portal, the fireworks surrounding it now only a tiny spark, and sent the picture to Flynn.

"What in the hell is that?" Flynn said. "Don't go in there, Jude. You don't know where that doorway leads."

"I have to go," I said as I reached for the magical gateway. "What if it doesn't open again?"

"Don't gamble with your life, dude. If you go now, you won't be able to return. Come home and we'll all accompany you."

I knew he was wrong. There was a reason the gateway opened for me. If I left now, I doubted it would open again. I only had one chance to see who was behind the portal.

"I'll try to be back by sunset." I ended the call when Flynn's colorful language rose in volume.

I pocketed my cellphone, pulled tightly on my backpack, and entered the portal.

Grab your copy...
www.vinci-books.com/jude

About the Author

A Multi-genre author writing twisted endings...

N Gray is a USA Today Bestselling Author who lives in Cape Town, South Africa, with her daughter and adopted cat named Miss Beans.

During the day, she's an analyst and provider profiler for a medical insurance company. At night, she types on her curved keyboard, creating fictional characters some may love and others you want to kill yourself.

She writes in four genres: urban fantasy, thriller, horror, and paranormal romance.

She now writes under Natalie Michaels for her new thrillers and SD Syns for her new horrors.

Acknowledgments

Thank you to my readers, old and new, for taking a chance on my books.

You are the reason I write the stories I do. As long as you keep reading, I'll keep writing.

I'm truly humbled by your support and encouragement.

I write in as many genres as I love reading in. There are so many stories swarming inside my head that I could never just choose one.

Horror is my guilty pleasure. I love writing short stories filled with dark humour and the occult, with a twist ending.

Urban fantasy and paranormal romance are where I love to spend my time, and I have so many books planned that I don't have enough time *(but I'll get there)*.

And lastly, my thrillers. Who doesn't love sitting on the edge of their seat while reading about what goes on inside the antagonist's mind? Well, I love writing about them.

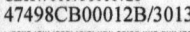